LEARNING TO CRAWL

by

JOHN ARGUS

Chapter 1

Gwendolyn Allison Pepperdine was more than mildly intoxicated. Even seated, the world appeared to her to be swaying pleasantly from side to side, much as it did on her father's yacht on a mild summer day in the English Channel. She found this to be an interesting diversion from the young man opposite her, who, despite rakish good looks, was a disappointingly dull companion.

It was not, as it chanced, a mild summer day. It was a rather chilly January in New York, and Gwendolyn Pepperdine - Gwen to her many friends - had excused herself from dull classes in art history at Oxford for a brief swing across the ocean. Her friend Desmond was holding a party in New York, and it simply wouldn't do to turn down his invitation.

Besides, Art History was proving to be as dull as Ancient History, Philosophy and Sociology had before it, and she considered it to be a waste of her precious time when she was probably going to change her major again quite soon. The professors were all arrogant overbearing twits, in any case, who had an anal-retentive fixation on punctuality and attendance.

Her normally soft brown eyes were somewhat glazed as she sat in the corner of the club, and her long brown hair was dishevelled, looking, as one of her girlfriends had remarked in amusement, as though she'd just been 'had'.

She was sprawled untidily in her chair, her short skirt riding dangerously high. By the time she took enough notice of the flashes of light to turn her head to frown at their source the photographer had drifted back into the crowd. She turned her head back towards her companions, disinterested.

The photographer was quite professional and the pictures, despite the poor light, came out bright and filled with colour. That they showed Lord Pepperdine's stepdaughter sprawled drunkenly at a table in a disreputable American nightclub, legs spread apart, her clearly shaven and panty-less groin fully visible, was not a source of arousal to him. He was a homosexual, as it happened, and only appreciated the money such a clear and revealing photograph would draw from the London tabloids.

As he developed each picture he clipped them to a rack above his counter, inspected them briefly for flaws, and gauged their monetary value. The last was clearly the best of the bunch, as Gwendolyn Pepperdine was looking straight into the camera. Her dress had a plunging neckline, and due to her position the top had fallen forward sufficient to give the camera a full and unchecked view of her right breast. It was a lovely breast, he thought, smiling pleasantly. It was full and creamy white, with a petit pink nipple. The shot of her groin would have to be blacked out in the family papers, but the breast could be shown in all its glory.

He smiled happily, and then reached for his phone.

Gwen hung up the phone, wincing and holding her head with one hand. Her stepfather had been furious, if the matter could be understated to such a degree. It was bad enough she had buggered off from school yet again when he was paying so much to gain her the education she 'needed', but to publicly humiliate him before his peers in such a fashion was beyond forgiveness.

Had she not been more than a little hung over she might have been able to placate him. Unfortunately, she'd been in a bad mood to begin with. Instead of apologising she had reminded him that 'his' money was, in fact, her mother's, that he had squandered 'his' money on a stock scheme which had gone into receivership shortly after she was born, and that had it not been for his good fortune in marrying her mother he would, in all probability, be making his employment as a shop clerk. As a result he had cut her off completely, or so he said. She'd get not a single penny more from him until she learned how to act like a lady and gained sufficient discipline to behave the way a Pepperdine was expected to.

She was not overly concerned with this, at first. Her stepfather made many idle threats and she had always before managed to wheedle and cajole him into rescinding them. When she found out later that day that access to her account had been cut off and all her cards cancelled she was less alarmed than angry, but a second conversation with Lord Pepperdine produced considerable invective on both ends, spoken with far more volume than thought behind it.

He wouldn't give her a pound until she begged him, actually begged him for his forgiveness. She must do so meekly, while admitting her utter inability to take care of herself. And she must accept his conditions for a return to the fold. These included no more drinking, no drugs, no partying, no wearing of 'revealing' clothing, and no more absenteeism from the law school he intended to enrol her.

The gall of the man!

Especially since it wasn't even his money! Of course, her mother was an absolute puppet to him and always had been. Her father had died when she was very young, and his cousin moved in quickly to 'help' her take care of things. The wedding followed as soon as decently possible, and he had been ruling the roost ever since. Gwen had long since given up trying to get her mother, a very weak-willed and fluttery woman, to ever disagree with any pronouncement of 'Lord Pepperdine'.

Gwendolyn was an intelligent but somewhat indolent young woman. Growing up in the lap of luxury left her disinclined towards manual labour. Furthermore, as a fortune awaited her the moment she turned twenty-one - a gift from grandfather - she had never felt any great urge to waste away her youth in mouldy classrooms listening to dried up old men and women lecture her on uninteresting topics, and was therefore without any academic credentials necessary to obtain any other kind of position. She promised her stepfather however, that it would be a cold day in hell before she came crawling to him for a thing, that she would have no difficulties, as an intelligent young woman, in supporting herself. He, in turn, promised her she would soon be on her knees

3

begging for money.

For the first several weeks Gwen managed to secure lodging with various friends and acquaintances, but as time passed this became more and more difficult; people stopped returning her phone calls. She was annoyed to find how many of her 'friends' lost interest in her once she no longer had money to spend, and had no intention of trying to phone across to her real friends in the UK and beg money from them. The very idea was simply too humiliating.

Imagine the gossip!

She then made some effort at obtaining a position, but even if she'd had the skills she quickly found she was not legally permitted to work in the United States. She had no money for a return trip to the UK, and most certainly was not going to call her stepfather to ask for some. In fact borrowing money, as opposed to lodging, from anyone struck her as a demeaning activity, and one with which she had no experience whatever.

Finally, with nowhere to lay her head, Gwendolyn Pepperdine stuffed her clothing into two lockers at Grand Central Station and tried to keep warm by wandering through the shops during the day and the clubs at night. She found herself getting more and more footsore and dispirited, and growing more desperate in her efforts to find lodging not accompanied by rats or insects.

The only beds she had been able to garner for herself had been those shared with men who were far more interested in parting her from her clothing than providing her with shelter.

She was growing weary and starting to feel more than a little frayed around the edges. Much of the confidence she felt when she boldly told off her stepfather was now gone and she had to wilfully suppress a growing feeling of being dirty and, what was more, cheap.

Her desire for a warm bed caused her to considerably lower her standards in the men she took as lovers.

It wasn't that she was terribly inhibited when it came to sex. She was, after all, or at least considered herself to be a sophisticate, a well-travelled cosmopolitan girl who was not subject to petty and culturally backward concepts about virginity or chastity. If she wanted to sleep with a handsome man there was no reason at all why she should not.

Still, sleeping with men in hopes of cajoling money or lodging from them made her feel like a cheap tart and beggar.

Gwendolyn was twenty years old. Her softly formed face was lovely and elfin sweet. Her small mouth was full-lipped, and with her snub nose gave her a delicate childlike look instantly denied by the piercing intelligence and sophistication in her large grey eyes. Her soft, chestnut hair fell across her shoulders like strands of silk, the curving bangs dancing just above her eyes. She was tall, with long, exquisitely formed legs. An artist could have sculpted her buttocks, and her breasts were high, firm, and only slightly oversized for her slender frame.

She had been aware since the age of sixteen that she could have virtually any man she wanted, and had long taken it for granted. She had not, of course, taken

4

advantage of her attractiveness to the degree she might have liked. It would not do to get a reputation. She knew too well what contempt and scorn was heaped upon the girls who did not meet the proper standards of taste and discretion as established by... well, her peers.

Still, she was experienced sexually. Even before coming to New York she'd had at least half a dozen lovers, and that, she was sure, was more than sufficient to initiate her into virtually every aspect of sexual conduct and behaviour.

She was trying a new club this night, and groaned in relief as she stepped in from the cold, her beauty buying her entrance where money would not have. Once inside she removed her long leather coat, fighting a small ripple of embarrassment. She was wearing a very short black velvet mini. It was little more than a wraparound square of material some twenty-nine inches in length. As her hips were thirty-four inches around the opposite ends of the strip of cloth were held together over her right hip by a stylish golden chain - at least at the top. The bottom remained dangerously loose under the intense scrutiny the scanty garment received.

Above her skirt Gwendolyn Pepperdine wore a short tight halter which was open at both sides, giving tantalising views of the soft creamy skin of the full young breasts thrusting outward against the material constricting them. That material was immodestly thin, and the delicate outlines of not only her small nipples, but the surrounding areolas were perfectly and clearly outlined to the casual viewer.

It was a daring outfit, one she had never before worn except to private parties given by friends whose sophistication and maturity could be relied upon. Wearing it at a public dance club gave her stomach odd flutters. She did not consider herself an exhibitionist, yet all those eyes, many without the sophistication to hide their lust, staring at her scantily clad body not only embarrassed but oddly, aroused her.

She was not certain why she felt as she did, and had little time for such considerations in any case. Her eyes looked slightly disheartened, and held a touch of desperation as she scanned the room. She expertly assessed and dismissed man after man as they settled briefly upon them. She had decided to search for an older man, perhaps one as old as thirty - and living alone. He would perhaps, at his advanced age, by so delighted at the prospect of touching her nubile young body that he would think nothing of allowing her to stay a few days at his apartment.

It briefly occurred to her, as it had more and more often of late, that seeking out a man who would foot her bills in exchange for sex was not far removed from prostitution, but she dismissed the uncomfortable thought. The distance was far enough.

She was looking towards the bar when a man caught her eyes. At first they passed him by, for he was far, far too old to even consider. Then her eyes were drawn back, for it was apparent he was staring at her. She frowned at him for his insolence, yet there was no embarrassment at all in him. He did not shift his eyes away guiltily as so many would have.

Instead he smiled lazily, and held up a glass in offering.

She snorted for a moment. The man had to be over forty, practically decrepit. Yet he looked very powerful standing there, with broad shoulders and no sign of a belly creeping over his belt. His clothing looked tailor-made, and his eyes held a strangely attractive strength - as well as something else. She found herself walking across the floor to him before she even recognised it.

It was danger. There was something very dangerous in this man's eyes, and it made her shiver a little as she stepped up before him.

His eyes looked down towards her breasts before rising once more to her face, but he said nothing.

'Like what you see?' She'd meant her tone to be cutting but it came out almost timid.

'It'll do,' he said.

She opened her mouth to respond angrily but to her surprise he brought his hand up, a finger pressing against her lips.

'Don't speak,' he said.

She felt indignation and anger, and yet snapped her mouth shut, frowning at him.

He examined her lazily, eyes moving down her body. She felt a strange sense of anxiety grip her as his eyes rose once more. She felt the oddest sensation, as if he were about to attack her right there, tear her clothes off and simply... have her.

'I have a car outside.'

She blinked in surprise, and then felt his hand on her arm, gripping it firmly, leading her away from the bar.

Again indignation rose within her. 'Look—'

'Be silent.'

She glared at him as he led her to the door, and then watched as he took her coat from the coat check girl and idly tossed her a hundred dollar bill. He folded the coat over his right arm as he put his left around her and guided her to the door.

She felt a rising sense of fear, yet with it was a strange feeling of respect for his strength and certainty. She had always admired strong people, people who knew what they wanted and went after it. She supposed that was partly a response to her weak-willed mother, and partly a reluctant appreciation of her stepfather's arrogance.

And yet this man wanted her. And she had no doubt as to why. Every step she took with him led her deeper into accepting that she was about to give him her body. A man she literally knew nothing about. Her stomach fluttered at the thought, yet her loins felt a soft throbbing arousal. What a bestial thing to do! To just let this strong stranger take her like that!

Her mind was spinning indecisively, caught between jerking back and making some kind of demand. Yet it seemed easier to simply do nothing, to let him guide her forward. His hand slid down onto her bottom and squeezed it lightly but possessively, and the soft throb in her loins grew stronger even as her anxiety rose.

The car was a large black Cadillac with dark smoky windows, and she looked nervously at the uniformed chauffeur before letting the man guide her inside.

She sat with as much grace as she could manage given her brief garments, and smiled with what self-assurance she could manage at the man twice her age as he slid in beside her. The chauffeur closed the door and hurried around to the front.

'Wait a min—' He put his finger against her lips again, his eyes dark and, she realised with a shiver, hungry.

God, what was she doing?!

His hand slipped along her cheek, caressing it lightly as she gaped up at him, and she felt her heart begin to pound as he leaned in to kiss her. She eased back slightly, but not much, knowing she was his, that she could not work up the strength now to push him back. She felt some instinct telling her she dared not anger him, but dismissed it. She was not afraid of him - at least, not very. She was simply looking for a strong man to give her shelter for a bit. And what had she to barter but her body?

She pursed her lips automatically, though perhaps a little shakily, her hands rising to slide over his shoulders. His kiss started softly, but not hesitantly. His lips caressed hers gently, surprising and pleasing her. Then they slid in more firmly, his tongue dancing along the edge of her lips. His body turned further in against her, pressing her back into the seat as the car started forward, and he kissed more deeply.

Her eyes fluttered with surprise at the force and expertise of the kiss, at the heat she felt starting to flood her body as his tongue slid into her mouth and his big hand came up to cup her cheek. His other hand slipped around her back and then into her halter through the open side, and casually cupped her breast.

She stiffened briefly, shocked by such quick presumption and aware of the chauffeur up front, but then slowly relaxed, stomach fluttering as more heat seeped through her mind and body. She was surprised to feel the rise of such excitement, to feel her insides begin to melt under his touch. She was no virgin, after all, and had been involved with a number of boys.

Boys, she thought weakly.

He was stroking her nipple, which had erected almost instantly, thrusting out like a small, quivering tongue into his nimble fingers. He twisted it enough to make her wince slightly, then rolled it between his fingers in such a way that a wave of liquid heat rolled through her body.

His lips trailed down the nape of her neck, his hand leaving her face as her head rolled languidly. She gasped aloud as she felt it slide unerringly between her legs, feeling a flush of embarrassment at the nearness of the chauffeur even while instinctively spreading her legs.

It was insane. It was too fast. He'd think her a cheap tart.

She pushed feebly at him but he ignored her, effortlessly pushing aside her uncertain hands and continuing to caress her body. He did not grope her as had so many of the others. His hand stroked gently along her inner thighs, caressing her skin to either side of her mons to the point where she felt a desperate yearning for his touch there. His teeth nibbled under her ear and his other hand manipulated her breast with an expertise that left her nearly breathless.

Finally, he eased a single finger upwards along the length of her moist opening, letting it sink slowly down between the lips of her sex, Then he drew it gently upwards so it stroked across her clitoris.

Gwen's back arched and she exhaled in an animal sound of lust. She had never before encountered a man with such skill in drawing pleasure from her body. Rather than pushing him back she was eager for him to continue, panting and gasping aloud, perspiration beginning to glisten on her forehead as her heart pounded and her pulse raced.

She looked over his ear as his lips worked down the side of her throat, and saw the lustful eyes of the chauffeur in the rear-view mirror. She knew a moment of awful shame, and then a strange twisted kind of shocking excitement. She was on the edge of climaxing under the man's eyes!

She couldn't do that!

And yet her hands resisted the thought to push him back, and her legs, while quivering, did not close at all. She slumped lower, further exposing her sex and knowing a shameful thrill as she realised the chauffeur would see her even more fully. True, there was a glass divider between them, but that did nothing to hinder his view, and the chauffeur, a large black man, seemed to have no reluctance at all in watching.

'P-please,' she gasped.

The finger continued to dance over her sex. He did not penetrate her, though she felt a longing for it, but instead stroked lightly up and down the length of her burning furrow. Each time it sawed over her clitoris she felt a new stream of soaring animal pleasure and her body shuddered in response.

'W-wait... not... not here...' Her hands pushed at him with more strength but again he ignored them, and his fingers thrust sharply at her sex. She gasped and looked again at the rear-view mirror as the chauffeur stared. She whimpered helplessly, closing her eyes, her head rolling from side to side as her hips began to buck against the hand.

It eased back and she was able to gulp several desperate breaths of air. Her head was pounding with surging waves of sexual energy, and with a slow shock that rippled along her frame she realised he had undone the chain binding her brief skirt together and was undoing the catch at the back of her halter.

The shock echoed in her loins and she felt the climax rising within her. Her frantic eyes shot to the mirror and the chauffeur, who stared hungrily. She was completely naked now, in the back of the limousine, legs spread, body fully exposed. The man's hand slipped back between her thighs and she came thunderously. Her body stiffened and then trembled like a tuning fork. Her back arched and her head pulled back violently, rolling against the top of the seat as her hips bucked whorishly against his hand. The orgasm seemed to hold her in its grasp for an endless length of time, her chest aching from lack of air, her muscles spasming and straining. Then it released her and she went limp, gasping for breath as the man slowly eased back.

She sat, slumped, legs apart, head back, naked, for long seconds, then as her shattered mind fit itself back together she weakly closed her legs and searched for her skirt and top.

Neither was to be found and she stared weakly up at the man, still not knowing his name.

'You have a lovely body,' he said.

She stared at him mutely, uncomprehendingly. The sexual thrall in which she had been held began to recede and with it the humiliation at her nudity and behaviour rushed forward to surround her. Her face went scarlet as she tried to cover herself with her hands, crossing her legs and darting her eyes about the interior of the car.

'You don't need to hide your body,' he said. 'It's something to take pride in, not shame.'

'Please, may I have my clothes?' she gulped.

'Why? I've seen you naked. Paul has seen you naked.' He nodded towards the chauffeur. 'What have you got left to hide?'

It was difficult to answer a question put with such calm logic, for her discomfort and embarrassment had nothing of logic in them. Now that her sexual high had faded she felt vulnerable without her clothing, under the eyes of two powerful, fully dressed men.

He reached for her again but her hands were before her, hiding her private parts in a way she knew was childish and foolish. That knowledge only embarrassed her more. Behaving with anything less than sophistication before others was the very last thing she had been willing to do for a very long time.

The car turned into a garage and the light immediately dimmed. Gwen looked around, then back at him smiling down at her. 'Why do you want to put clothes on now?' he asked. 'You'll simply have to remove them in a minute, anyway.'

The car turned and then stopped before a gate. The gate eased aside and they drove through into a small, private part of the garage. The car stopped and he opened his door, stepping out with her clothing in his arms. He stood there, the chauffeur joining him, as Gwen shrank back flustered and embarrassed and then angry, both at him and at herself.

'Come on, no need to be embarrassed,' he said with a smile.

She mustered what dignity she could and slid forward out of the car, doing a poor job at hiding a glare as she deliberately held her hands at her sides, naked apart from her heels.

The chauffeur was inches away and her skin seemed to heat at his hungry gaze as she stepped forward. The man took her hand and led her to the doors of a lift, smiling lightly. She ignored the coolness of the air on her exposed flesh, desperately trying to pretend she was fully clothed.

Behind them the chauffeur pulled away in the car. The gate leading to the outer garage opened, then closed behind him.

Gwen's stomach began to flutter anew as the man's arms went around her, his hands caressing her stomach, then rising up to cup her breasts. She looked nervously at the gates, which while keeping other cars and people away would do little to hide sight of them should people drive up.

The lift doors opened and she jerked in surprise, but he only chuckled. 'It's a private elevator, my dear,' he said with a smile.

He motioned her forward. She swallowed nervously, but her insides were beginning to thrum with heat once more, and she stepped forward into the lift.

The walls were mirrored, and naked Gwendolyns looked back at her from all directions as the doors slowly closed. She stared at them in fascination, embarrassment, some anxiety, and no little excitement, doing her best to show none of the emotional turmoil she was feeling.

'Tough one, are you?' he asked, smiling faintly.

'You're very good with your hands,' she said accusingly.

He nodded. 'You're very responsive.'

'Will the rest of your servants not be surprised if I show up naked?' she asked nervously, watching him fold her little skirt and halter and slip them into his jacket pocket.

'I like the place to myself, for the most part. The cleaning ladies come in every other morning while I'm at work.' His hand slipped down to fondle her bottom, and she felt a little thrill of wickedness run up her spine. Then she remembered with a trace of anger and disappointment that she had to attempt to cultivate his interest in order to gain a place to stay. She was so tired of wheedling people for shelter and food she was almost ready to give up and call her stepfather.

'W-what's your name?' she asked.

'Why?'

'Well, I...'

He turned her to face a corner then pulled her bottom back against his groin. His fingers ran up the front of her body, briefly fondled her breasts, and then drew her hands high above her head. He joined her wrists together, much to her puzzlement, holding them in one hand, then used the other to push into the small of her back, thrusting her chest out as he drew back her arms.

There was a small camera high in the top corner of the lift. She stared at it uncomprehendingly for long seconds, feeling a shock run through her. Then she instinctively attempted to twist away and hide from it.

She remembered the sight of herself in that tabloid newspaper, right on the cover. One of her 'friends' had eagerly and laughingly shown it to her, suggesting she had a possible career in men's magazines. She had felt mortified at the sluttish image she showed to the world, and it had taken every ounce of will she held to maintain her dignity and project an uncaring face. 'Don't... please,' she gasped, hips twisting from side to side.

He held her steadily, his lips moving in along her earlobe. 'Do you have any idea how many men are watching you now?' he whispered.

Another shockwave rippled through her, and she struggled more frantically.

'Spread your legs for them. Give them a show.'

'Stop it. Let me go!'

He chuckled but held her in position. 'The camera only goes to my penthouse,' he whispered.

She blinked and felt immense relief, though she continued to stare at it uneasily. 'No one is... watching it?'

He chuckled. 'Not unless they've broken in.' He eased his hand back while holding onto her wrists, then turned her so her buttocks pressed back against the mirrored wall. His other hand slid down, teasing her nipples, plucking and rolling them until both were throbbing. He grinned at her as she swallowed nervously and looked away, then let a finger lazily slide down her belly and in between her legs. 'Do you think I can make you come before we reach the penthouse?' he asked.

'Of course not,' she said, her voice slightly husky.

His fingers caressed her mons once more, this time his index finger slowly and gently penetrating her, pushing up inside her moist tunnel to the knuckle. A second joined it, and the two began to caress the inside of her as his thumb worked over her clitoris.

'Of course, I could be lying,' he said. 'Perhaps there are men watching, dozens of them.'

She gasped, unable to stop her eyes from darting to the camera again. 'You... bastard,' she said with a gasp.

He grinned and she tried to stifle her reactions to his fingers. 'Spread your legs.'

The words, so cool and demanding, sent a little sizzle of heat into her groin, and she obeyed without thinking, looking up at the camera again as his fingers began to stoke the fire inside her. She imagined a gang of men watching, perhaps security guard types at a desk below. Perhaps he had lied to her and even now her sluttish behaviour was being observed. Her hips began to undulate slowly, and her breasts rose and fell with growing speed as his fingers manipulated her sensitive flesh.

'Do you want to come, girl?'

'Please I...'

'Do you want to come... on my fingers?'

'Oh... oh, I can't!'

'Do you?'

His hand held her wrists high above her, and her buttocks rolled and ground against the cold glass of the mirror as his fingers sawed against her sex. 'Y-yes,' she whimpered.

'Yes what?'

'Make me come,' she panted, grinding her buttocks against the wall.

'Beg.'

She stared at him in confusion, and his thumb pressed against her clitoris.

'Beg to come,' he ordered.

'Ohhh...' She twisted but he held her easily in place, and then relaxed his thumb, his fingers no longer moving.

'Beg.'

She glared at him, wanting to deny him but needing the pleasure more.

'Please,' she said, fighting to force the word out.

'Please what?'

She felt her face warming. 'Please make me come.'

'Let me hear some emotion, my little slut.'

She inhaled sharply as his thumb began to stroke her clitoris again. '*Please* make me come,' she groaned.

'Louder.'

'Please make me come!' she cried, and felt the strangest sense of release as she did, panting heavily as she ground against his fingers.

'What a naughty little girl you are,' he said, his hand shunting between her thighs almost violently now, and she let out a startled cry as he began to masturbate her quickly and roughly. His fingers sawed over her sensitive clitoris and thrust sharply up into her body, the knuckles almost punching against her soft mound. It hurt at first and she felt the beginning of alarm and fear, but then the pleasure exploded within and she lost control of her body. Her hips rolled and twisted as she jammed herself desperately against his fingers. He released her wrists and she almost fell, slumping back against the wall. He caught her hair painfully, jerking her head back as he crushed her lips with his. She threw herself against him, whimpering, moaning and crying in pleasure. Her leg rose and curled around his waist as she ground herself against him.

The lift doors opened and he bent, grasped her about the waist and lifted her up across his left shoulder like a bag of potatoes. He carried her out and down a long polished corridor into an enormous bedroom with sweeping, panoramic views of the city below.

She was flung on the bed without ceremony and she lay there, gasping, as he stripped.

Most of the men she knew socially were young, slender, pale, and had little incentive to subject themselves to much strenuous physical activity. This man was different. He had broad shoulders and was powerfully built. His suntanned body was lean but muscular, with a long diagonal scar across his chest. He looked... rough. He looked nothing like the soft young men she was used to.

She felt a new thrill. Here was a powerful man who would take her and use her!

He stripped off his trousers and pants and her eyes moved eagerly to his erection, rising high and firm from the tangle of dark pubic hair between his legs. 'Fuck me,' she said with deliberate crudeness.

'You're a real little whore, aren't you?' he said with a sardonic smile.

'Yes. I'm a whore. Fuck my brains out.'

She spread her legs wide and he crawled between them, then he knelt over her, reaching for the top corner of the bed. He drew out something soft and she raised her eyes to look as it wrapped around her wrist. She felt and saw the leather cinch tightly, and a sharp throbbing excitement began in her groin. 'W-what are you doing?' she asked.

'I'm going to tie you up.'

She stared at him, gaping, her insides twisting at this dangerous idea. 'Why?'

'So I can do what I want with you, of course.'

The words were shocking, and yet the excitement within her burned brightly at the words, and she closed her eyes.

He then strapped her other wrist to the opposite corner of the bed. Then he turned his attentions to her body. His fingers resumed their deft manipulation of her senses and were soon joined by his tongue, stroking teasingly against her quivering nipples as she pulled against the straps.

'Bite them,' she groaned.

He mouthed her right nipple and areola, chewing on the surrounding flesh. She groaned in a mixture of pain and pleasure, trembling as he sucked rhythmically. His tongue rasped across her nipple as it throbbed within his mouth.

He drew back, holding her nipple between his teeth, grinding them from side to side so that she cried out weakly. Then he was licking his way down slowly between her legs. She thrust her hips up at him and he pushed them back. A moment later her ankles, spread lewdly, were strapped to the lower corners of the bed and the man proceeded to drive her mad with his careful, expert tonguing.

There was a mirror above the bed and she could see herself there, spreadeagled, body writhing in tune to his fingers and tongue. The idea of a mirror over the bed would have drawn howls of laughter from she and her friends; only a crude fool would do such a thing. But she did not laugh as she saw herself; she stared, transfixed, mouth open.

He was above her then, blocking the mirror, holding her face tightly between his large hands.

'Fuck me,' she breathed.

'Beg for it.'

'Please fuck me,' she moaned.

His hands glided over her body and squeezed her breasts, and then he seized her nipples between thumb and forefinger and pinched sharply.

'Owww!'

He stretched her nipples up, twisting them from side to side. 'Say, sir.'

She looked at him dazedly.

'Say it.'

'Sir,' she whispered.

He released her nipples, guiding the head of his erection to her yearning opening. 'Again.'

'Sir, fuck me,' she panted. 'Use me... use me hard and *ungghhhh...*'

He drove himself into her with a single, brutal thrust that hurt, but after the initial shock and pain she drove herself up to meet him. Her ankles pulled against the straps holding them down as she tried to draw her legs up around him. The sensation of being pinned down was wicked and spurred her arousal even higher. 'Yes... yes... ohhhh...' She climaxed beneath him, her pussy spasming around his savagely rutting cock, aching from the force of his thrusts even as ferocious pleasure consumed her.

13

The orgasm was overwhelming, and she fell limp and slack-jawed as it finally left her.

She lay still beneath him as he continued to use her body, grunting mildly as he drove into her again and again, body jerking in time to his thrusts, fingers twitching feebly above the binding straps.

He finished and lay briefly atop her, then rolled off, sat up and walked away. But she did not care. She groaned weakly, looking up at her reflection in the mirror, then smiled lazily at herself, arched her back a little, posing, eyes gazing at the straps holding her ankles and wrists with interest and excitement. She pulled at the straps, watching the movement of her body, imagining herself a helpless prisoner struggling against lewd, evil men. Strong men. Men capable of anything. Men like this one.

Chapter 2

He wandered into the room, holding two glasses. He'd put on a pair of shorts, and looked quite impressive to her still hungry eyes.

He sat on the edge of the bed and set one of the glasses down on the bedside table.

'Bastard,' she said challengingly.

'Why?' He ran his free hand casually over her body and she swallowed and brought a stern look to her face.

'Sir?' she demanded.

'It's a good word,' he replied, his fingers pinching her nipple lightly.

'Do you think I'm your servant or something?'

He smiled and she felt a sinking sensation, wondering if she was being far less subtle than she thought. It occurred to her that at twenty she might not be quite as sophisticated as she thought, at least compared to a man old enough to be her stepfather. 'Would you like to be?'

He plucked an ice cube from his glass and held it over her. Cold droplets fell onto her breasts, sending little shocks through her overheated body.

'Don't,' she gasped.

'Servants don't give orders,' he said mildly, then lowered his hand to her chest, the ice cube held against her body, then slowly, lazily, slid it down between her breasts and then up once again, circling her left breast as she writhed on the bed, letting the ice cube ease inward until it was sliding back and forth across her straining nipple.

'It's t-t-too *cold*,' she moaned, arching her back and straining against the straps.

He smiled and drew the cube back, then let his finger circle the stiff pink nipple. Small goose bumps were standing up on the pale flesh around it, and her areola was studded with tiny bumps. He bent and covered the area with his mouth, sucking softly, his tongue teasingly lapping across it.

'Christ,' she breathed, closing her eyes briefly.

'Would you like me to keep you chained here for a while?' he asked, smiling lazily.

She blinked and tried to concentrate, remembering her primary reason for approaching him in the first place. 'I ah, as it happens I just got into town,' she said weakly. 'I don't have a place to stay yet.'

He snorted, and then chuckled lightly as his hand moved between her legs and she hissed and arched her back as the ice cube slid up her furrow, then popped lightly inside.

'You were pointed out to me, you know.' He pulled the ice cube back, and after a moment to process his words she stared at him in confusion. 'You think no one knows?' Gwen tried to keep her face from showing any response as he grinned down at her. 'Papa cut off his little girl and she's now looking for a sugar daddy to keep her until he relents.'

'Don't be absurd,' she said feebly.

He leaned in and trailed his lips over her nipple, then brought his eyes to within inches of hers. 'If I drive you home now where will you go? What address will you give me? Central Park?'

'I have money,' she said weakly.

'Want me to drive you somewhere?'

She did not answer.

'You haven't got the money to pay the door charge at any of these clubs. If you weren't so cute and they didn't let you in for free you'd be begging on the streets.'

'Untie me,' she demanded, falling back on her custom of acting imperiously when embarrassed.

'Not so fast.'

'Untie me at once!' she snapped.

'And what will you do if I don't?'

She stared at him. Not do it? But of course he must. How could he not?

'Perhaps I'll just keep you here and use you again and again and again. How does that sound?'

'You will release me at once,' she said, as calmly as she could manage.

His fingers slid down between her thighs, and the muscles moved beneath her skin as she instinctively sought to twist away. She was still chilly there from the ice cube, and exquisitely sensitive.

'Stop it,' she demanded, but his fingers manipulated her sex with careless ease, and she felt her body begin to respond. His other hand moved up over her breasts, stroking and kneading, rolling her nipples between thumb and forefinger.

'It's so cold outside, isn't it?' he teased. 'It's freezing out there.' His hand moved from her breast, then returned with one of the ice cubes.

'*Oh...*' it sizzled against her nipple as he rubbed in slow, taunting circles. Drips of water rolled down the curved surface of her breast, changing course as her back arched and twisted.

'Imagine living here with me, letting me ravish you night after night, living in the lap of luxury.'

Her nipple was so cold it burned, and then the ice was gone and his mouth replaced it, massaging gently, the tongue caressing lightly. The cold seeped away and her nipple, deliciously sensitive, throbbed and glowed within his mouth.

'Wh-what are you doing to me?' she moaned.

'Nothing,' he smiled innocently. 'I wouldn't want to do anything against your will. Come to think of it, you wanted to be untied, didn't you?' He pulled back, then casually and quickly undid the straps binding her wrists and ankles. 'Get dressed,' he said, 'you can leave now.'

He picked up his glass and left the room as Gwendolyn sat up, staring after him. She felt astonished at his sudden departure, resentful, indignant, and, she admitted, sliding a hand down between her legs, extremely aroused.

Damn!

She thought about what he had said, mortified at the thought that people knew, that they had been watching her and whispering about her, that they knew not only of her poverty but of her attempts to find someone to let her stay with them. And now she'd irritated this strange man and he was throwing her out.

She almost cried, and felt her eyes filling even as she rose from the bed. She could not go back to those clubs - not now, not ever.

That realisation stopped her cold for a moment. The only alternative seemed to be calling her stepfather and admitting she was useless, helpless and still too much of a child to look after herself.

The man's jacket was draped over the arm of a chair. She went to it and yanked out her mini, then slid the small square around her hips and clipped the chain in place. She pulled on her halter and, shrouding herself in dignity, strolled arrogantly out of the bedroom.

The penthouse was enormous. The floor and walls of the corridor outside were of polished marble, with crystal globed lamps set into the walls. Her heels clicked on the floor as she made her way to the end, and there found herself before a railing overlooking what she supposed was the main room.

She was desperate to convince him to let her stay, but she could not ask, would not ask. It would be too degrading. She should leave; simply get in the elevator and go. But she could not bring herself to do so. Instead she stepped down from the entrance hall and moved as casually as she could manage across the room.

The floor to ceiling glass wall at its end overlooked a terrace almost as large as the room, with trees and flowerbeds scattered along one side, and a group of ornate iron tables placed against a chest-high wall. He was standing by the glass doors, looking out, and she strolled over, unable to keep her eyes from straying to the magnificent view.

'How high are we?' she asked unwillingly.

'Fifty three floors.'

A forest of skyscrapers filled the world around them, most much lower than they. Gwendolyn felt as though she were in a cloud.

16

He turned and looked at her. 'Weren't you going?'

'You sound like you want to get rid of me,' she said with a weak laugh.

'No, I just thought you wanted to leave, to get back to... wherever.'

She blushed. Rotten arrogant bastard! 'I didn't say that. I just...' she was caught by a lack of words.

'Had to be getting back home in case you missed curfew?'

'I don't have a curfew,' she said cuttingly.

'No? Finished high school already?' He smirked.

'You weren't treating me like a high school girl in there,' she countered defiantly.

'How do you know how I treat high school girls?'

She shrugged casually, looking out the window.

'You aren't very sophisticated about sexual behaviour, are you?' he went on.

She looked up in surprise, and then blushed as she considered his words; did he think she wasn't any good? That would be simply too humiliating! 'What do you mean by that?' she demanded.

'When I put on the straps you seemed... shocked.'

'I wasn't shocked,' she said defensively. 'I was just... a little surprised. I mean, I don't often get tied to a bed.'

'You were aroused by it,' he observed.

'Maybe. So?'

'I think inside that mask of sophistication you wear is a teenage virgin with big round eyes.'

'Don't be ridiculous!' she snapped.

He reached down and casually raised her skirt and she flinched back, gasping, staring at the window. He raised his eyebrows. 'Afraid someone will see you?'

'Well... well yes, actually,' she said indignantly.

'And so what if they did?'

Damn, she was acting like a child, and then it occurred to her that she'd never had anything much to do with older men. They were, after all, her stepfather's sort of people. Why on earth would she want to be around them? And yet obviously they had to be more sophisticated, at least in some ways, merely for having been around longer. Yet the idea of being seen as unsophisticated, as common, was anathema to her.

She stepped back, glowering up at him. 'I don't see you dropping your trousers to show everyone what's inside.'

'Ah, but what I have inside isn't nearly so lovely. And it's only impressive when it's awake.' He smirked a little, and then reached around to unhook her halter. She started to react, then stopped and let him. It dropped to the floor and he reached to caress the underside of one breast.

'You still haven't told me your name,' she gulped.

'Yes, I have.'

She thought back in confusion, but could recall nothing.

'Sir,' he said. 'And your name is?'

'My name is Gwendolyn,' she said with a scowl.

17

He shrugged and took her arm. 'Let me show you the place.'

He took her arm and led her through the living room and down a second hall. It felt quite odd to her to be walking about without a top, but then she'd done it before, hadn't she? In France, at the beach the previous two summers. Yes, and hadn't many people seen her, too? So this was surely nothing to be bothered by; a sophisticated woman wouldn't think twice of it.

And the penthouse was all he had described. There was a billiards room, a movie theatre, several small sitting rooms, a library, a greenhouse full of colourful flowers with another marvellous view of the city, and a swimming pool, half of which was within a glass wall, the other half outside on another large terrace. There was a sauna, whirlpool baths and gym, all of them brightly lit and decorated, with large glass windows.

And then he led her into another room. It was an inside room, with no windows, and the walls were of heavy, gleaming mahogany. Chains hung from the ceiling, and frames with attached straps and shackles were spread around the room. There were shackles set into the wall, and posts with attached chains set into the floor.

On one wall was a rack that contained an astonishing variety of whips, flogs, quirts, canes, straps and paddles. Set into it on a shelf beneath was leather bondage devices, and on a second shelf were dildos and vibrators.

Gwendolyn was awed at first, then frightened. She turned and gave him a nervous look. 'Your own little torture chamber,' she said uncertainly.

'Yes,' he said simply. 'You were looking for a place to stay.' He motioned to a cage set against the wall.

'Oh no,' she said, shaking her head. 'I think not.'

He chuckled. 'Oh, I don't expect you to sleep here, or even spend much time here. I brought you here because I think you're a natural submissive and I think we could enjoy each other's company a good deal.'

'I might find being... being tied up a bit of a kick, on occasion,' she said warily, 'but I've no intention of being whipped or anything like that.' But even as she spoke she felt a strange sense of disorientation. What would it be like to be whipped? She looked at one of the chains and imagined hanging by the wrists, naked, being beaten.

'What about spanked?' he asked, cupping her bottom through the short skirt.

'Absolutely not,' she snorted and jerked away, but he took her suddenly, swinging her round and pushing her against a low table, then bending her forward.

'Stop it!' she shrieked. 'Let me go!'

He tugged her skirt undone and she felt the cool air on her buttocks. 'What a beautiful sight,' he whispered. 'You have one of the finest bottoms I've ever seen, my dear.'

Indignation warred with pride, but both were outdone by alarm as a hand caressed her buttocks. 'Don't you dare hit me,' she warned, trying again to twist away, but he simply gripped both her wrists, lifted them up behind her head and held them there.

'Are you afraid, Gwendolyn?' he goaded.

'I-I'm not afraid,' she said indignantly.

'You look it,' he mused. 'The thought of being spanked is terrifying you, isn't it?'

'Don't be ridiculous,' she snorted unconvincingly.

'It doesn't scare you?'

'I don't like pain,' she said. 'That doesn't mean a spanking frightens me.'

The hand slipped between her legs and cupped her sex, then began to slide in and out between her thighs, rubbing her. She wanted to curse him but instead found her legs shifting apart.

'What is pain but heat?' he said. 'And what is pleasure but heat? How do you tell them apart when they arrive at the same time?'

Was he crazy?

The hand moved back.

'Spread your legs,' he ordered flatly.

'I - I won't...'

'Spread your legs,' he barked.

She flinched and then obeyed, surprising herself.

'Lovely,' he said. 'This is you in all your glory.' He let go of her wrists, but she did not try to rise.

'Lift your bottom a little,' he directed. 'Yes, perfect, you could charge for this view.'

He was disgusting! Yet she felt the heat within her flickering back to life. She had been so close to coming again before he untied her and now she was blatantly open and exposed to him, lewdly displaying herself before a man as old as her stepfather whom she'd barely met!

'You want me inside you, don't you, slut?' he said.

Slut? How dare he?

He laid his hands on her hips, then slowly, gently, stroked up her sides to her ribs, his fingers easing under to massage her breasts. Gwen fought to control her breathing, but had little success.

Then a hand cracked lightly against her bottom and she yelped at the sharp pain, jerking upright. He folded his arms across his chest, looking at her without expression as she glared and rubbed her bottom.

Here was a dangerous man, and she felt a dark excitement at the thought.

'I could stay...' she motioned back at the open door, 'in your penthouse?'

He nodded.

'As what?'

'As my guest.'

'Your guest?' she asked doubtfully.

'My obedient guest.'

'Obedient? And what if you did something I didn't want? I mean, what if you wanted to... to spank me and I said no?'

'Use your finger to push the elevator button and then walk away,' he answered simply, and even as she felt a slight fear at the idea of placing herself at his

19

mercy, she felt a strange dark excitement matching it.

She would be a captive to his lusts, a prisoner, chained and used.

What wicked things would he force her to do? How often would he use her body to satisfy his perverted male lust?

The idea was insane of course, and he was crazy. And yet...

'Of course, you'd have to earn your keep,' he added.

'Earn...? How?'

'By carrying out any order I give you, be it to clean the floor, fetch my cleaning, or... service me.'

Service him?

'I'll not punish you too severely. But you will obey my every word and show me the proper degree of respect. Do you understand?'

'I guess so, but—'

'Say, yes sir.'

She stared at him for a long minute. It was a beautiful apartment, and she could stay in idle comfort for some time. 'Yes, sir,' she said, barely breathing the words.

He smiled, then withdrew a folded sheet of paper from a pocket and placed it on a low table, placing a gold fountain pen beside it. 'Sign this,' he ordered.

'What is it?'

'Never mind what it is. Sign it.'

But of course, she couldn't simply sign something without reading it:

I, Gwendolyn Allison Pepperdine, agree to being employed by CLF Enterprises Incorporated, in the position of Body Servant. In this position I agree to obey any and all orders given, and to provide the full use of my body in any way, sexual or otherwise, my employers desire. I consent to any punishment, physical or otherwise, my employers choose to exercise.

'But, I can't sign this!' she blurted angrily. Although she had a suspicion such a document was invalid, she knew little about law. Her head span; when had he prepared it? And how did he know her full name?

'Sign it or leave,' he said firmly, breaking into her confusion.

I acknowledge that my lack of skills, talents or academic credentials makes my most reasonable employment that of a sexual pleasure device and will endeavour to fulfil this duty to the best of my limited abilities.

'This can't be legal,' she declared.

'Then sign it.'

Gwendolyn pursed her lips, pondered for a few seconds, and then signed the paper. He took it and the pen from her and put them away.

'Now put your hands behind your head and arch your back,' he ordered. 'More, slut... that's it.' He circled her slowly, examining her body, and she stood there, feeling her arousal growing. She had never displayed herself for a man before. It felt bizarre.

He moved away, and then returned. 'Take this,' he said.

She saw he held a large realistic looking plastic phallus, and took it awkwardly.

'Put it inside yourself.'

She stared at him in shock, then gasped and dropped it. 'I can't do that,' she said.

'Why not?'

'I... well... um...' She did not know how to answer him, so he shook his head slowly and she blushed in confusion as he picked up the dildo and put it in her hand.

'Do it now,' he insisted. 'Show me you can obey when I give you an order. Don't argue. Don't question. Just do what you're told, you little whore.'

She stared at him, shocked and anxious, then looked down at the phallus and inhaled sharply. Knowing she had to obey she placed it against herself, and immediately felt a surge of response at the pressure against her sex. She blushed more deeply, looking down at the plastic device as she slowly forced the lips of her sex apart.

'Look at me,' he ordered.

She raised her eyes, feeling a shameful pleasure at performing such a degrading act in front of a virtual stranger. She eased it into her body a little at a time, and each time her eyes moved off him his harsh voice ordered them back.

'All of it, slut,' he ordered ruthlessly.

She knew he was using the harsh words deliberately, wanting to shock her. And yet they struck that same dark hidden part of her mind, which created a heat that set her legs trembling.

'It's too long,' she pleaded.

'All of it,' he said adamantly. 'Every inch.'

She moaned, twisting the thing slightly, pressing the base. The tip was high inside her. She could take no more, and trying sent a spasm of discomfort through her abdomen.

He stepped forward and slapped her hand away, then held the monstrosity, shifting the angle of penetration as he thrust. She cried out as it was pushed up deeper within her; pushed up until the flat of his palm pressed against the hot flesh of her mons, then gave her a squeeze.

'You have to learn to know the female body,' he said in arrogant amusement.

He moved to the shelf and lifted off a pair of leather restraints, then quickly strapped her wrists together behind her back. A collar followed, to which he attached a leash. Then he led her from the room and along the hall. Gwendolyn's mind was awash with contrary impulses. She was worried about his intentions and indignant at his treatment of her. At the same time she was finding a strange, wicked delight in the very things that worried and angered her. It was so deliciously kinky and nasty. No one had ever treated her like this, and she was finding it deeply arousing on a level she had not known she possessed.

He led her by the leash into the front room. 'Kneel,' he ordered abruptly.

21

She obeyed, breathing raggedly as he stood before her.

'Sit back on your heels and spread your knees wide. Keep your back straight.'

'Yes, sir,' she whispered. It was a silly game, of course, but deliciously exciting.

He dropped the leash and sat in a plush antique chair, staring at her, forcing her to meekly drop her gaze. 'How many men have you fucked, Gwendolyn?' he asked.

She raised her eyes again, frowning. 'None of your business,' she said.

He reached for her leash and yanked her forward, then grasped her arm, hauling her up across his lap so her bottom was raised high. 'That's the kind of rudeness that demands instant punishment,' he said.

'But you were rude first,' she protested.

His hand settled on her rear. 'I am the master. You are the servant. Do you understand that, slut?' His hand cracked down against her bare bottom and she yelped.

'Yes,' she panted.

'Obviously you will have to be spanked for such rudeness.'

She said nothing, her body flaring with heat, her mind spinning anxiously. His hand cracked down again and she yelped once more, the pain flaring briefly before fading. Again he spanked her, and again, and she tried to keep from making a sound. Indignation rose as she was swamped in excitement. What would her friends think? The girls would be so jealous and—

'Ow!'

'Naughty little sluts cannot be permitted to speak with such insolence,' he scolded. Her bottom was getting warmer and warmer as the blows landed in slow, measured progression. It hurt, and Gwendolyn had never been one to seek out pain. Yet the little shocks of each blow rippled through her belly and down through her groin, and she moaned as she clenched her thighs together, squeezing her pubic muscles around the long thick plastic phallus deep inside her.

The blows came faster, really stinging now, and she winced and yelped and promised him her obedience. She could see nothing, her upper body being bent down over his lap, her head lolling just above his ankles.

Then the blows stopped and she was left gasping and panting.

'Spread your legs,' he ordered calmly.

She obeyed meekly and his hand cupped her sex. She could feel she was wet, and knew a new source of embarrassment.

'What a slut you are.' His voice dripped with contempt and alarm took her briefly. Then she realised he was speaking so on purpose.

'Yes, sir,' she whispered.

He squeezed her a little painfully, then softened his grip and let his fingers stroke her slit. She moaned, helplessly thrusting back at him. He tapped the base of the dildo embedded within her and she felt the vibrations echoing deep inside her belly.

'Do you want to come again, slut?' he asked.

'Yes, sir... please make me come, sir...' she groaned.

His other hand slapped down hard on her throbbing bottom and she yelped and jerked. 'I'll do as I choose, slut.' His fingers resumed their stroking and tapping and she moaned as the pleasure swept through her.

Another sharp blow on her bottom made her squirm. He resumed his stroking, bringing her to the edge of a climax. Then his hand slapped down, not on her bottom, but on her sex. The pain was different; duller but deeper, and she made a strangled gasp as it hit the wall of sexual heat surrounding her mind.

'You were made to be a sexual plaything, Gwendolyn, to be at the beck and call of any man who wants your body.'

The words aroused her, and she squirmed breathlessly. And then he started stroking again and her bottom was grinding weakly once more and the pleasure was rising to nearly unbearable levels.

Again he slapped her there and again she cried out in pain and denial, but his fingers soon stroked the pain away and once more her body was thrumming with sexual energy.

And again a sharp smack on her sex brought her back down to earth. She let out a sob, not so much for the pain but the loss of the climax that had been so near.

He was playing her like a violin, with an expertise she had not imagined any man possessed. She would go mad if forced to remain in such a feverish state of sexual need for very much longer. She felt dazed, her body moist with perspiration, her insides aching.

Her wrists twisted weakly within the bonds holding them, and reminded her again of her helplessness - of the wicked, kinky nature of her position.

She felt the climax approach once more with a desperate yearning. She tried to keep her body from giving evidence, hoping to sweep into it without him knowing. It came closer and closer, until this time she was sure she would reach it. This time he was going to permit her to feel the final release she so craved. The beginnings of it swept around her, and then his hand cracked down against her vulnerable sex in a sharp flurry of blows.

The climax receded briefly at the first blow, then surged forward once more, growing and growing like a massive wave, pouring over her with shattering power.

She screamed as it hit her, shaking and grinding violently, head lolling back and forth as the climax caught her up and sent her flinging into a wild maelstrom of sensory pleasure.

She could dazedly feel the sharp pain slicing into her body, yet somehow the pain was transformed, or absorbed, and each new blow was like a burst of sexual electricity, throwing her higher and higher into a storm of mindless ecstasy.

The orgasm was still shaking her when he shoved her off his lap onto the floor. He dropped down, gripping her hips and pulling them up, raising her bottom, then kneeing her legs apart. With her face pressed against the rug, jaw slack, eyes gazing without seeing, he slipped the phallus out and fed his cock into her.

He gripped her hips tightly, yanking her backwards to meet his savage thrusts. His groin struck her buttocks with powerful slaps as he rutted wildly inside her. Her breasts and face and shoulders jerked back and forth on the rug as he grunted like a brute, using her furiously.

Chapter 3

Gwen slept in his bed that night, but with her wrists bound behind her back and her ankles locked together. She woke during the night, finding his hand between her legs, fingers lightly stroking her sex lips. She came softly, groaning weakly as he sniggered beside her.

Then she felt him moving in the darkness, saw his shadow rise beside her as his hands moved along her legs. They gripped her calves and lifted her bound ankles high, then pushed them back so that her knees pressed into her breasts. Kneeling there, he thrust his erection into her and, nothing more than a panting shadow overhead, used her briefly but roughly before dropping her legs once more and going back to sleep.

This would show *daddy*, she thought. She was reduced to being a sex toy to a nasty, nouveau riche yank!

She woke in the morning with him, briefly confused, then recalled her situation and felt a new blossoming of arousal as she pulled at the bonds holding her wrists together. He was stirring beside her and she caught his eyes as he turned to look at her.

His eyes were cool and calculating, measuring her, perhaps assessing her body. He threw back the sheets to show he was as naked as she, and then gestured to his penis. 'Show me what you can do with that mouth besides talk,' he ordered.

She should have been outraged. How dare he talk to her like that?

But instead she felt a little dagger of heat between her legs. 'Yes, sir,' she whispered meekly. She sat up with some difficulty, and then rolled over until her face was over his thighs. She licked at the head of his cock, and then took it into her mouth, sucking softly. Almost immediately she felt it beginning to throb with life. She sucked the rest of the flaccid organ into her mouth and massaged it there, and then as it began to stiffen she drew her lips back slowly until only the head remained inside. She let it pop free and lapped at his testicles, and then took each into her mouth in turn, licking and sucking and massaging with her tongue.

He was hard now and she took him into her mouth again, sucking as she bobbed her head up and down. She was in an awkward position without being able to use her hands or arms to support herself, and her neck was beginning to ache. So she shifted positions, bringing her knees together beneath her then bending forward. Again she took the head into her mouth, lapping at the underside as she sought to please him.

His hands fell to her hair, stroking it as she bobbed up and down. He came and she swallowed his sperm, licking faster as he groaned and squeezed down on her head. He began to soften and she continued licking, but then he pushed her off and sighed, laying there comfortably, bringing his hands behind his head.

'Well now,' he said, eyeing her, 'what should we do with you today?'

'Anything you want, sir,' she challenged.

'Breakfast.' He stood up and pulled on a robe, then gestured towards the door. Gwendolyn waited for him to undo the snaps holding her ankle restraints together, but when there was no indication he was going to she threw her legs out of bed, prepared to hop.

He shook his head. 'Crawl,' he said.

She looked at him in confusion for a moment, and then eased down onto her knees. She could not, of course, crawl while her wrists were bound behind her but—

'On your belly,' he ordered curtly.

She felt a fluttering in her stomach, and then awkwardly lowered herself to the floor until she lay on her stomach. She began to crawl forward, grunting as her breasts were ground beneath her body, trying to raise her chest somewhat to ease the pressure on them. She made slow progress, gasping and grunting with every wiggle that moved her forward.

And so they moved down the marble hall, the naked young woman wriggling on her belly, bound ankles sweeping from side to side behind her, hair trailing over the floor, gasping and panting, and the older man walking patiently alongside, wearing an expensive silk robe and smiling enigmatically.

They passed the lift, Gwen tiring rapidly from her exertions and wanting to ask him to let her walk. She knew he would not, however, and deep within knew that would spoil the wickedness of what she was doing anyway. So she continued, wriggling, rolling from side to side, toes pushing against the floor as her breasts were rubbed and rolled painfully along the hard, cool marble.

They moved along the second hall, and then turned in at the kitchen, moving across the tiled wood there until they reached a table. She gasped then as she felt his fist in her hair. He yanked her head up painfully, though not unbearably so, lifting her upper body off the floor and pulling her back onto her knees. There he had her sit on her heels and wait.

He started making breakfast, and Gwen, out of breath, aching in a variety of places and chilled from the floor, watched, panting and excited.

She was completely caught up in the 'game' now, wanting to play her part of helpless, imprisoned girl fully. The smell of the sausages he was cooking made her mouth water, and her throat was dry. But she made no requests for food or water, knowing as his virtual pet she would be fed and given water when her master decided, and not before.

'We'll have to find something for you to wear, I suppose,' he said after a few minutes.

'My things are in a locker at Grand Central Station,' she volunteered, but he glanced at her with annoyance and she realised she had done something wrong. Perhaps she ought not have spoken.

'We'll fetch them, but I doubt you'll be wearing any of them. I had in mind something else, something less... restrictive.'

'Restrictive?' she said with an uncertain laugh. 'Compared to these?' She twisted to the side, displaying her bound wrists.

'Are you arguing with me?'

'No sir,' she said quickly.

He frowned and walked over to her. 'You have a lot to learn about showing your master the proper degree of respect due.'

She gave him a deliberately insolent look. She had been aroused since waking and remembering she was bound, and he had done nothing to assuage those feelings. Perhaps she could goad him into spanking her again.

He walked away, and the kitchen counter blocked her view of him as he left the room. She could hardly follow, so she knelt, feeling a combination of wicked anticipation and wary fear. What was he going to get? A paddle, perhaps? Would he paddle her? How much would that hurt?

He returned holding, so far as she could see, nothing, but walked over and squatted beside her. 'New servants always seem to want to test their masters, to see what they can get away with,' he said, and then cupped her breast, pinching and plucking the already hard nipple.

'I'm sorry, sir,' she apologised.

'You'll say that with more sincerity soon,' he promised with feeling. Then she saw he did hold something in his hand. It looked like a small golden ball, attached to a short golden chain that had a tiny clip at its end. He pinched on the clip, opening it, then placed the little jaws around her nipple. She inhaled sharply, and then cried out as he let it snap closed.

'Owww...' she wailed, jerking from side to side. 'It hurts... please take it off,' and her sudden defensive movements made the heavy little ball dance and tug on the end of the chain, pinching her nipple even more fiercely. He ignored her and produced a second ball and clip, and despite her protests, quickly snapped it onto her other nipple, before returning to his cooking.

Her cries and yelps soon dropped to winces and gasps as she looked down at the things. The initial sting had been terrible, but had settled quickly into a sharp little throbbing ache.

She glared at him, wanting to demand he remove them. Yet the worst was over, though they continued to throb uncomfortably. And she had been deliberately goading him.

She winced again, trying to hold still so her movements did not make the little balls jerk and tug. 'I'm sorry, sir,' she said sincerely, but he did not reply. 'Please take them off me, *sir*...' she pleaded, but he merely turned and glowered at her again, shaking his head.

'Do not ask for a punishment to be rescinded,' he said coldly. 'It will only draw more punishment. When you act up and are punished, learn your lesson and don't act up again.'

Gwen said nothing; he had set the rules and she had agreed to them. She was at his mercy so long as she remained. And running begging to her stepfather was no longer the main reason she wished to stay, she realised. In spite of the occasional pain she was finding it all deeply exciting and arousing. At that moment the thought of leaving, to return to her old life of relative boredom, was not at all attractive. All those boys who had fawned over her: what milksops they were compared to this man.

She sat quietly as he continued making breakfast, then watched as he brought a large plate over to the table beside her and sat down to eat. She did not ask for food, though she hoped he would make her something, or let her make something for herself later.

'Hungry, slut?' he asked suddenly, and another little shudder struck her at the word.

Slut. What a slut she was.

'Yes, sir,' she replied honestly, so he cut off a piece of sausage and, with his fingers, held it down to her. She looked at it in surprise, then swallowed a little wave of sexual heat and opened her mouth as she leaned forward. The weights tugged at her nipples, making them ache even more, but she ignored them, letting her lips close around the piece of sausage and take it from his fingers, then chewed quickly and swallowed.

Her chest tightened as she watched him; she was eating out of a man's hand!

If he did it again, she decided, she would lick his fingers. The thought made her squeeze her pubic muscles on emptiness and wish she had the dildo he had driven into her the previous night.

He held out another piece and again she leaned in, her lips sliding along it and brushing his fingers, licking at them as she took it and ate. Her upper body jerked a little more abruptly and the weights bounced on the end of the chains, making her nipples pulse.

The next piece he held out was in the palm of his hand, and she licked it off, her tongue sliding out, lapping slowly across his hand before she closed her lips on the meat. It was good, but she hardly noticed the taste; so caught up was she, so enthralled in her own submissive, degrading behaviour.

She passed her breakfast that way, eating bits and pieces from his hand. Then he set out a bowl of milk and she bowed forward, the weights dangling to the floor as she drank like an animal, bottom raised, legs apart. She wished he would take her again - hard. But he let her finish drinking before removing the bowl. He clipped the leash to her collar then and bent behind her to unclip her wrist restraints from each other.

'On all fours,' he ordered. The words shocked her and she hesitated, remembering the fiery and furious response she had made to the last boy who'd wanted her on all fours. But she swallowed her former feelings and, feeling exceedingly sluttish and wildly wicked, dropped onto all fours and let him walk her down the hall towards his dungeon. The weighted balls tugged much more severely at her nipples, swinging back and forth beneath her as she crawled, and she winced at the sensations but made no attempt to remove them.

27

Her heart began beating faster and faster as she realised his intent, and her mind span as she tried to think of what he would do to her. She was not ready to be whipped - was she? No, of course not. She would definitely not permit that.

'Stand,' he ordered, and she obeyed without question. 'Step over here. What do you think of this?' He led her before an X-shaped frame. With straps at the top and bottom of the wooden beams it was obviously meant to hold someone, and more than that, for a large polished wooden phallus was attached where the beams crossed, angled up at an acute angle.

'It - it looks... strange,' she ventured.

He moved to it and fiddled with the wooden cock until it came down and off. Then he motioned her forward. Gwen felt nervous but excited, and stepped up to the frame, facing it, reaching without being told for the top corners. He strapped her wrists into the restraints, then spread her legs and locked them to the bottom. She felt deliciously erotic as the muscles of her thighs strained, and then gasped as she felt his hands near her sex. He held the wooden phallus, and she hissed as he slowly pushed it up into her pussy. She was moist and ready, or the thickness of it would have hurt. Even as it was she ached a little as it spread her wide.

'On your toes,' he ordered, giving her bottom a smack.

She raised herself onto her toes and felt the thing being manoeuvred and attached to the frame. He moved around in front of her then, smiling from between the top arms of the cross. He released the two clips simultaneously and she cried out at the sudden rush of pain. That pain grew rapidly as the feeling returned to her nipples and she gasped and winced and pulled against her restraints.

Then his mouth closed over one of her nipples. He did not suck, but merely mouthed it, letting the inside of his mouth massage it gently. The feeling against her quivering, aching nipple was intoxicating. Both were so sensitive she could feel the gentle breeze from the air conditioning vent as it blew across them, and she whimpered in pleasure and pain as he moved his mouth and fingers from one to the other.

She eased down onto the wooden dildo, grunting as it slid deeper inside her. But there was a price to pay, she realised with a gasp. The thing was at such an angle that the lower her pussy lips slid the less space there was between the dildo and the frame, and just near the base was a little nodule on the frame which, by accident or design, ground directly over her clitoris.

He straightened, and then produced a golden chain. At each end was a small loop, which he proceeded to slip around her engorged nipples and then tighten. The loops did not hurt, as the clips had, but did hold tightly to her nipples. He pulled back on the chain at its centre point and fixed it to a small hook in the wall, then moved away.

'I have to shower and get ready for work,' he announced. 'I can't stay around here all day playing with you. Try not to get into any trouble while I'm gone.'

The door shut behind him and she was alone; surely not for the whole day. But the thought was brief; she had more important things on her mind.

She indulged herself by pulling at the restraints, reassuring herself she was a helpless prisoner. Then, too randy to resist, she began to carefully work herself up and down on the wooden dildo. It was difficult and her feet and legs soon began to tire as she slid up and down its length. But excitement leant her energy. As she moved her breasts shook lightly, pulling against the chain binding her nipples and sending wicked little sensations through her. She moaned, riding faster still, needing to take as much of the dildo as she possibly could manage.

She tried to avoid the little bump, to take only so much and then stop as she felt its edge. Her moist sex lips squeezed tightly around the thick phallus, sliding wetly up and down as she grunted with pleasure.

Gwen looked up at the wall before her, to where the chain was hooked, and saw the mirror there to one side. She had hardly noticed it before and hardly noticed it now, except that she caught sight of movement in it, and as she stared she realised it was reflecting the far larger mirror on the wall behind her.

That mirror reflected the lewd image of her rounded bottom working up and down, showed the glistening wooden phallus appearing and disappearing as she rose and fell. She stared at that hypnotic image, unable to tear her eyes away, hardly able to credit how intensely lewd and arousing it was.

She slid her sex down the dildo and groaned as she went too far, as the little bump ground across her swollen clitoris, pinching against it. She pushed herself up onto the balls of her feet and then onto her toes, paused, and then slid down again.

Too far... she groaned again as the nodule pressed over her clitoris. It hurt, but the discomfort was only a brief distraction from the flood of sexual steam filling her mind and body. She continued to ride the thing, growing frantic with heat and need, staring at herself in the mirrors, gasping each time she slid too low; which was every time now, for she needed absolutely every inch inside her.

She cried out as the orgasm hit her, only to discover instants later that it was only the prelude. The real climax tore into her then and she screamed, shaking violently in her bonds, riding the dildo with the last of her strength, sobbing in pain and wildfire pleasure as the climax rolled on and on, then faded, and then bloomed anew.

She had never before experienced multiple orgasms. She'd heard girls boast of it but considered them liars. Now a fleeting and shocked recognition struck that part of her mind still capable of thought as another orgasm gripped her, as she began a rollercoaster ride up and down a parade of them, body shaking and jerking, legs and feet working desperately.

In the end she collapsed, utterly exhausted, almost hanging by the wrists against the frame. He returned, neatly dressed in an expensive suit, smelling of expensive cologne. He smiled as he unlocked her from the device and settled her on the floor, and then walked out.

Gwen lay there for some time, exhausted and sore. Her feet and her calves ached, the muscles overstrained. Her pussy was feeling little better after the wild ride she had taken on the wooden phallus.

She managed to get to her feet and stagger out of the room, then along the hall to flop on one of the padded chairs in the main room. There she lay for a while, massaging her legs and feet and rubbing her nipples, which were still intensely sensitive.

She realised he was gone, and therefore had some time to recover and settle herself. She found an enormous green marble bathroom and filled a large sunken tub with hot, soapy water. Then she lay back and relaxed, idly stretching her legs and arms, letting the hot water work on tired muscles.

Gwen could hardly believe she had met the man not much more than twelve hours earlier, and that she had experienced so many mad sexual thrills in such a short period of time. She luxuriated in the penetrated warmth of the water, and in her new self-image as a wild, kinky, wanton slut. None of her girlfriends, she was sure, had ever enjoyed such an incredible experience. How they would drool when she told them!

It was so wildly perverse and thrilling that she was unsure she could even tell them the whole of it. It was strangely desirable to be a 'slut' here in this penthouse, with him, but that did not mean she wanted all her friends back home to think of her so.

What else would he do to her? In what other ways would he punish her and use her?

She let her legs spread under the water, drifted a hand gently down to her mons, and traced the line of her sex. She was sore, inside and out, and was amazed at the way she behaved on that rack, like a depraved animal, and wondered if she mightn't have a little of the nymphomaniac within her.

And of course, he was a beast every time he entered her, pummelling her mercilessly, rutting like a wild boar. She'd never had a man use her with such violent passion and utter disregard for her.

She let her finger stroke across her clitoris with the gentlest of touches. It felt sore, and almost raw, but was also beautifully sensitive.

Much like her nipples. They had stung awfully at the time, yet something inside her had deliberately made her writhe and pull on them again and again. And with each sharp ache had come a sizzling jolt of sexual electricity that made her breasts swell deliciously.

Gwen hissed lightly as the soft pad of her index finger gently rubbed against her clitoris. At the same time she rolled her nipple between a pair of soapy fingers. She groaned and spread her legs wider, slouching lower in the tub and raising her knees. She felt a pleasant tension in her inner thighs as the tendons stretched, and she slid all but her knees and head beneath the water. Her hands stroked and circled her breasts as her mind replayed the events of the morning, and the previous night. Each wicked highlight sent a little shudder through her mind and body as she added more pressure from the finger stroking her clitty. A finger slid gently inside, then stroked in and out as she remembered how he had thrust so harshly into her body. Her eyes closed and after long minutes of stroking she climaxed once again, sighing aloud.

She rested, relaxing, feeling drained.

After her bath she found nothing to wear but one of the towels, tucking it around her chest as she set out to explore the penthouse. It was a slow, intriguing exploration. The penthouse was not large compared to her stepfather's manor, but for an apartment in downtown Manhattan it was simply enormous.

She walked through the living room, despite her earlier climaxes still gripped by a simmering sexual arousal, then back to his bedroom and began to poke about inquisitively. In one drawer she found a pair of green silk pyjamas. They were too large for her, of course, but she rolled up the sleeves and it did for a nightshirt.

The rest of his clothing was predictably expensive but appeared, as far as she could determine, to be off the rack rather than tailored. She sniffed disdainfully and headed back up the hall.

The swimming pool was superb. It extended out beyond a glass wall onto the back terrace. She could see the mist rising from the pool outside into the chilly winter morning, and suddenly felt an almost overwhelming desire to swim under the wall and outside.

She hesitated, looking at the buildings nearby. None seemed quite as tall and she decided that, barring someone having a telescope, she was likely safe from close observation.

Dropping the pyjama top on a chair she gently eased down into the warm water. She swam slowly out into the middle, then with a kick and a dive went under, swam forward and then surfaced outside. The air was warm from the mist coming off the pool and she swam to the far corner, then climbed the steps and got out, gasping as she walked away from the warm air over the pool and felt the deep chill of winter bite her.

Yet she did not turn back - not immediately. She felt wild and wanton there outside, overlooking the city, nipples erect, goosebumps breaking out on her pale flesh as she moved carefully to the edge of the terrace. The air cut into her, freezing the water on her skin, and she knew it would be delicious when she did turn and dive into the warm water. She crossed her arms under her breasts, rubbing at the cold, and moved along the rail, looking out at the city below.

She lingered further, delaying the pleasure that awaited, growing colder still. She raised her arms, pulling back her hair, twisting it so that water, still warm, dribbled down her back and between her buttocks. Her feet were freezing and she imagined it as a punishment from him - from her master. She bent forward, consciously spreading her legs, raising her bottom as she tried to look all the way down to the street below. She looked down into the myriad of windows around her, watching the tiny forms of movement within, people working, doing boring office type jobs, she mused, copying this and dictating that.

Her breasts were so chilled now they were practically numb. She wondered if anyone was watching, and raised her hands to cup and squeeze them, but she could take no more of the cold and turned and jumping into the water. The warmth enveloped her chilled flesh and she groaned in delicious comfort, drifting slowly towards the glass wall, swimming easily then ducking beneath and coming up on the other side.

Why couldn't her stepfather have a place like it in London instead of that boring old barn in the middle of nowhere?

Gwen drifted slowly and then climbed gracefully out. There were towels on a shelf nearby and she dried herself, then put on his pyjama top once more and resumed her exploration. She bypassed most of the rooms, though she did spend a while in the little theatre examining his storehouse of videotapes. Then, finally, she headed for the strange torture chamber, fascinated, a low hum of sexual excitement still gripping her.

She took down and examined various whips, crops and paddles, sometimes lightly striking her palm, or hip, glancing irrationally and anxiously over her shoulder in case someone was spying on her. Then she tried to place herself in the various and outlandish frames. For some reason the chains thrilled her. She imagined hanging from her wrists, moaning - a picture of submission abused by her cruel tormenter. She raised her wrists, looking at herself in the mirror on the far wall, wondering what it would feel like to be hung so.

She picked up a ball-gag and fed it experimentally into her mouth, buckling it at the back of her head, then again looked at herself in the mirror, putting her hands together behind her back.

A sexual prisoner!

She trembled with arousal and moaned through the gag, and that brought a new thought and she moaned more loudly; she had always felt an instinctive need to suppress her sounds of pleasure from her lovers. There was a need for dignity and reputation had to be considered; a girl who uttered indelicate noises during sex lacked class, and a gag would help her maintain her decorum.

She removed it, and worked her stiff jaw as she examined the selection of sex toys. She had never imagined she could find such a wide selection of artificial penises. Some were white, some pink, and some black. Some were thin, some terribly thick, some were a few inches long, some looked like they had been modelled after horses. She was too tender to try them out, but she told herself she would eventually, then resumed her tour of the place.

She entered his bedroom and began to go through his drawers and cabinets again, trying to get more of an understanding as to what kind of a person her 'master' was. Finding a photo album helped somewhat. It showed him on various horses and out at what she realised was an oil-drilling platform. He wore a cowboy hat or hardhat and dirty jeans then. He was pictured with other rough looking men, drinking beers together or leaning against fence posts or pipelines. She wondered if oil was how he had gained his wealth. There were no pictures of women, which she thought odd.

His office contained a variety of reports and documents, few of which she could understand. She wished then that she had given some thought to those business classes her stepfather had often urged her to take. Perhaps there was something in what he had kept prattling on about after all. She did, however, determine his name at last.

'Ian Richardson,' she said, tasting the sound of it.

The name seemed so normal for such an odd sort of a man.

Chapter 4

Gwen went into the kitchen and made herself a snack, then went to the tiny theatre and spent a while playing with the controls of his satellite dish, trying to figure out how it worked. Eventually she was able to get something to watch and felt quite at home as she sprawled back in a comfortable chair and sipped a glass of wine.

'I don't recall giving you permission to use this.'

Gwen yelped and almost fell out of the chair. 'I - I didn't think you'd be home so soon,' she blurted.

'Obviously.'

'Well, I'm not doing any harm am I?' she said defensively.

'Sir,' he reminded her uncompromisingly.

'Sir,' she echoed obediently.

'And take that off at once,' he said, indicating the pyjama top with his eyes, his tone harsh and cold.

'Yes sir,' she gabbled, hurrying to obey. 'I'm sorry, sir, but I had nothing to wear.' She peeled it off immediately, feeling a sense of menace even as the low hum of sexual heat grew in strength.

'Then you ought to have remained naked,' he said simply. 'I think women like you should be kept largely naked anyway.'

'Yes, sir,' she said meekly, not really understanding him.

'Come here.'

Breathlessly she hurried over to him and he took her arm, leading her out and along to the main living room.

'Ouch,' she squealed, and jumped as a hand cracked against her bare buttocks.

'Don't ever presume anything, slut,' he warned. 'You will go nowhere and use nothing unless I give you permission.'

'Yes, sir,' she panted. 'I'm sorry, sir. I'm new at being a... a servant.'

'So you are,' he acknowledged, and then pushed her belly against the back of a chair, then bent her over.

Crack! His hand swept down hard against her raised bottom and she jerked sharply, crying out in pain. She tried to rise but a firm hand on the back of her neck shoved her over again as his hand came down in a fast tattoo, cracking repeatedly against her vulnerable bottom. The pain hit her from one side and the humiliation from another. To be beaten in such a manner made her feel like a naughty child. Of course, bent over and revealing herself as she was, was far from childlike, and that was an entirely different sort of embarrassment. Her buttocks warmed quickly and she yelped repeatedly at the stinging pains rippling through her body.

At that moment Gwen did not feel as though she was playing a game. In fact, it felt as if she really was being spanked. And it hurt!

Then he was pulling her up again, casually, with no regard or respect. She felt badly used in that moment and swung at him, tears in her eyes. 'Bastard!' she hissed with venom.

He swung her round roughly and again bent her over, pushing down between her shoulders, jamming her face against the seat so that her toes could barely hold contact with the floor. Again his hand began to rap against her bottom, harder still, and she sobbed in frustration and pain, twisting and wriggling. She tried to claw at him but he simply pulled both her wrists up and pinned them with one hand, then resumed the spanking. Her bottom was on fire, the burning intensifying with each new blow.

'Stop it! Stop it!' she screamed pitifully.

He yanked her upright again, still holding her wrists. 'Do you want to go home to daddy?' he demanded coldly.

Gwen sobbed helplessly, but shook her head. He gripped her hair and forced her head back, making her back arch. 'Are you going to stop acting like a spoilt little girl?'

'I... I...' She only wanted to protest that he was hurting her, but was too flustered and upset to get the words out. Besides, it wasn't just the pain, she knew. It was the casual infliction of it outside the sexual games; outside the thrilling excitement his knowing fingers gave her. It felt too much like, well, like punishment.

Which was entirely silly, but still outraged her.

His strong hand forced her to her knees and he glared down at her as she fought to control her sniffles. 'Do you think you can just do what you want around here?' he demanded. 'Do you?'

'No,' she said weakly.

'Do you want me to throw you out so you can go peddling your little ass around the clubs again?'

She hadn't done that - or at least, it wasn't like that.

It was all so very unfair, and his hand shoved her forward and down until she was lying on the floor. He knelt beside her, still gripping her wrists and hair, pushing down so that her face was forced against the floor.

'You're about as high as that,' he sneered. 'An inch off the floor. You should thank me for anything I do to you.' He let go of her and stood up, but then his foot came down against her back, shoving her down just as she started to rise. 'Who is your master?' he demanded icily.

'Y-you are,' she whimpered.

'And I can do anything I like with my servant, can I not?'

She grunted with the effort of breathing with his foot pushing down on her back. 'Yes.'

His foot lifted and he caught her by the arm, wrenching her up so quickly she stumbled and almost fell. A quick slap to the face sent her reeling back, but then he embraced and held her tightly. 'Are you going to be a good, obedient little slut?' he asked quietly. She stared at him dazedly, and he shook her. 'Are you?'

'Y-yes, sir,' she said with a fragile voice.

He let go of her after a final shake and she slumped. 'Go and fetch me a drink,' he ordered.

Gwen stared at him uncomprehendingly for a moment, then gathered her wits and turned away, moving to the bar as he sat down. She rubbed her buttocks ruefully, wincing slightly as they throbbed. She felt very much like a humbled girl, glancing resentfully over the top of the bar at him as she searched out the bottles. He hadn't had to spank her so hard, after all. And it wasn't fair!

Accepting the drink he pointed down and, blushing slightly, she dropped to her knees so he could study her while he drank.

'Have you remembered your manners?' he asked.

'Yes, sir,' she said quietly.

'Then bend over that,' he nodded at the coffee table.

Gwen felt a new surge of anxiety at the instruction, but turned slowly and leant forward over the low piece of furniture, laying her soft breasts against the enamelled wood.

'Now I want you to spank yourself,' he directed.

She blinked at him in astonishment.

'Now. If you don't like me spanking you, you'll have to do it yourself.'

Her bottom was still hot and tingling from his spanking, but she fought down a protest. Complaining that her bottom hurt would be too... too childish. So Gwen reached back awkwardly and spanked her own bottom.

'You call that a spank?' he said, voice dripping with contempt.

She bit her lip and spanked harder, wincing as her backside flared hotly.

'Harder, you miserable little bitch!'

She spanked harder, whimpering at the pain, for it was twofold; her buttocks hurt, but so did her pride.

'Faster,' he demanded. 'I want to hear nothing but the slap of flesh on flesh.'

Somehow it did not occur to Gwen to refuse. She spanked herself faster, trying to ignore the heat in hand and bottom, as well as the indignity of what she was doing.

'Enough,' he said finally. He produced a collar and leash and then led her, crawling on all fours, back along the hallway. Gwen moved hesitantly, the floor cold on her knees, her bottom on fire. She felt a great sense of relief that her punishment seemed to be over, but was still gripped by resentment at the way he treated her, and confusion about just what she could do about it.

He led her back to the small dungeon room, and across the floor to what she had taken to be a small table. He whipped back the cloth covering it and she saw it was, in fact, a cage; a very small cage, but made of strong metal bars. It was less than two feet in width and height, and not very much longer. One end had a small round opening, and the other opened completely.

He unlatched the opening end and ordered her inside. She crawled in reluctantly, not at all surprised to find it too small for her to fit entirely within. But then he was at the other end, unlatching the upper half and lifting it away. He motioned her forward and she reluctantly obeyed, so that her head protruded out of the end. He pushed down on her head until her throat was pressed into the bottom half-circle, and then slowly brought the top half down onto her neck so that her head was inextricably locked in place. He moved back to the other end of the cage and closed the door, which pressed firmly against her bottom and forced her to shift her feet apart and raise them slightly.

Gwen heard him continue to work at that end, and then yelped slightly as something pushed against her. She tried to shift aside but was only slightly successful as her room for movement within the cage was minimal.

'Hold still,' he ordered.

Again she instinctively tried to look back, but with her neck caught in the hole she was unable to. She could feel something cool pressing and shifting until it rested against her sex. Then it pushed forward and she knew there was little point in trying to evade it. Instead she concentrated on relaxing her muscles as the thing, a dildo of some sort - hard and chilly as steel - pushed deeper and deeper into her soft warmth.

It was thick, but not much thicker than his erection was, and though hardly aroused she was able to accommodate it with little difficulty. A moment later he appeared once more, and to her surprise he placed a padded blindfold over her eyes.

Her hands were free, but the strips of metal were too closely fitted to get more than a few fingers through, thwarting any hopes of removing the blindfold. She reached back instead, sliding a hand between her thighs and feeling the thing inside her. It was thicker than she had thought, and definitely metallic. Her fingers traced the tightly clasping lips of her sex as they gripped it, then moved along the metal dildo to where it seemed fixed to the rear wall of the cage. She tried to move it, but to no benefit.

She sighed and assumed the most comfortable position she could, given the circumstances, letting her head fall and bracing herself on hands and knees.

Gwen considered herself sophisticated, but this sort of sexual punishment, if punishment it was, evaded her understanding. In truth she really had no greater understanding of what aroused and seduced people than most girls her age. The fetishes and perversions which interested those not within the mainstream were more than a little beyond her understanding. Not in any fantasy or nightmare had she ever imagined anyone would place her in a cage, nor would it have ever occurred to her to purchase such a cage - as he had done - for the purpose of imprisoning others. It was a truly bizarre thing to do, and she was feeling more than a little put out by it.

On the other hand, she was a young woman who had recently been exposed to the wicked joy of being dominated and used, and in that light being caged in such a manner did make her feel aroused.

The rise in heat was slow in coming, awaiting the fall of the annoyance and pique gripping her. Once that gave way to boredom, however, she began to slowly experiment with the only likely source of diversion within her cage. She found she could slowly push herself backwards until the metal which encircled her neck was jammed against her jaw and the base of her skull, and that in doing so her warm pussy could swallow several additional inches of the dildo.

She reached down between her thighs once more, now mildly excited, and began to gently rub her clitoris as she worked against the metal dildo. The heat began to rise much more quickly, and she was soon gasping excitedly as she rode back and forth along the now warm, slick metallic tube.

Her first realisation that he was still present came with the snap of clasps holding part of the cage together. It was not the front part, nor the back, for they remained firm. But moments later she felt his hands gripping her wrists and pulling both up and behind her back. He said nothing, merely handcuffing them together there. Then she heard a clang of metal on metal as the cage was closed once more.

Having been startled - and embarrassed - by his sudden presence she held still, trying to tell if he had left. Her new position was considerably less comfortable than her old, for without her hands to hold up her torso her back was beginning to strain, and she soon had to lay some of her weight on her throat as it lay clasped in the hole. With some effort she worked herself forward so that her shoulders were propped against the front of the cage, and held herself like that for some minutes.

But then, certain he had left, she began to work herself backwards again. Despite the strain on her back she began to grind onto the metal dildo, gasping with the effort as well as the pleasure.

Then she heard the sound of the snaps being released again and cursed mentally, halting her motions. 'Sir?' she asked in a breathless, quavering voice.

He did not reply. She felt straps being placed about each thigh, and then grunted as they were pulled backwards, the pressure digging the leather into her soft skin as they pulled her sharply onto the dildo. Her head was pulled back against the hold to the point of pain as her jaw wedged in tightly. Then she felt the pipe pushing forward.

'Ungghhhh... that's too deep!' she cried, but there was no reply. She heard the sound of the cage being closed, and again there was silence. 'Sir...? *Sir...?*'

Her head was caught painfully tightly now, and she could not move forward to release the pressure. Nor could she lean against anything to support her upper body. Her back was forced to hold her in that uncomfortable position, for she could lay only a small amount of pressure down on her jaw where it was trapped inside the hole.

The dildo was deep within her now and she could do nothing to release that pressure either. Aside from twisting her wrists within the handcuffs or wriggling her torso a little she could not move at all. 'Sir?' she called again.

Her insides throbbed uncomfortably with the pressure of the dildo, but her back was by far the more painful problem. She called several times for him, promising to be good and apologising for her misbehaviour, but was answered only by silence.

It was difficult to tell how long she remained caged in that fashion. It seemed like hours though she eventually discovered it was much less. A finger along her jaw wakened her to his presence and she babbled her apologies again even as the finger slid along her lips and then eased within.

'Do you want to please me, slut?' he asked.

'Yes,' she cried.

His finger pressed against her tongue and began to slide in and out of her mouth. 'Show me.'

Her confusion was brief, and she closed her lips around the finger, licking as he pumped it slowly in and out. She sucked desperately, eager to show him her remorse that he might release her. One finger became two, then three, and she slurped and licked at them, heedless of the indignity, caring only about the pain and discomfort gripping her.

The fingers were withdrawn and his penis rubbed her cheek. She opened her mouth submissively and it pushed between her lips and slid over her tongue. She closed her lips around it and sucked, her tongue pushing up against the underside as he pumped lazily in and out.

'You'll do anything I tell you, and you won't complain,' he said.

She tried to nod in agreement.

'You're not a weak little girl, are you?' His tone was of irritation and scorn. 'You're an adult. You embarrass yourself by losing control over something as trivial as a spanking.'

She blushed a little, for of course he was right.

His cock continued to slide steadily in and out of her mouth and she worked on it as capably as she could, hoping the pleasure she gave him would cause him to relent and let her out of the cage, but then her mouth filled with his viscous spending without warning, and after a moment of surprise she swallowed, feeling his organ beginning to soften between her lips.

He withdrew, and moments later she felt the cage opening. He undid the handcuffs and then released the straps binding her thighs. The front part of the cage came up and he slipped off her blindfold. She saw then that the entire top of the cage came open as well, and heaved a sigh of relief as the metal dildo slid backwards and the pressure on her insides disappeared.

The back of the cage was opened up and she backed out, groaning as she was able to straighten up. She fell onto her side, arching her back and stretching in every direction. The relief was wonderful and she felt a wonderful sense of languor spreading through her body.

She gasped only slightly when he knelt and began to tease her clitoris, spreading her legs, drawing back her knees and grinding against his fingers as she continued to writhe in sensual delight. Sexual heat built rapidly and soon enveloped her in a steamy sense of delicious pleasure. Then he stopped and rose to his feet and she felt a deep disappointment as he moved to the wall. But then he returned, holding a thick plastic phallus.

She spread her legs in anticipation, and groaned in delight as he slowly pushed it into her. It was thicker than the metal probe, and much softer. It slid easily into the soft moist flesh of her pussy, and a moment later it was fully within her, the flat of his hand pushed against the base to force even that inside her, almost.

Perhaps a quarter inch protruded, holding her pussy lips tightly open. She luxuriated in the deep penetration; the feel of it was so very much softer and gentler than the unyielding metal had been.

But then he seized her arms and lifted her back up onto her knees. He moved to a corner cabinet and opened it, and she blinked in surprise to see a small television monitor. On a shelf above it was a video recorder, and atop that...

'Oh no, wait,' she gasped.

'Getting shy?' he mocked, taking down the video camera and setting it before her. Gwen stared at the unblinking eye of the thing anxiously, then turned to look at the television, which was showing her what the camera was recording. For the moment it was focused on her head and shoulders, her breasts below the level of the screen.

'Tell us what a little slut you are,' he coaxed smoothly, utterly in control of the situation.

She stared at him, then at the camera, swallowing nervously.

'Um... I'm not sure I—'

'Are you a slut?' he persisted.

She inhaled deeply. 'Yes,' she whispered.

'Louder.'

'Yes.'

'Say it.'

She hesitated. 'Yes I - I am a slut,' she said.

'A whore?'

'Yes, I'm a whore and a slut,' she breathed.

'Describe your present position.'

'I - I'm on my knees.'

'What else?'

'I'm naked.'

'What else?'

She felt her chest tighten, and glanced sheepishly at the monitor. 'My hands are bound behind my back and... and...'

'Go on.'

'And I have a large dildo inside me,' she blurted.

'Where inside you?' he taunted.

'In my vagina,' she said.

'Your cunt.'

Gwen closed her eyes in shame. 'Yes.'

'Say it.'

She took a deep breath, and repeated, 'Cunt. I have a dildo in my cunt.'

'And have you been punished recently?'

'Yes,' she admitted faintly.

'How were you punished?' His questioning was relentless. Gwen had nowhere to hide.

'I was spanked,' she said.

'Why were you spanked?'

'For wearing your pyjama top,' she said, trembling slightly. 'I'm not allowed to wear clothes, and certainly not yours.'

'Because you are here as a sexual toy.' It was a statement rather than a question. 'Because you enjoy being a sexual toy.'

'Yes, I enjoy being used as a... as a... What are we doing here?' she asked plaintively.

'Whatever I decide,' he said simply. 'Tell me what you were doing on that frame this morning.'

He nodded at the X-shaped frame and then panned the camera that way.

'I was tied to it,' she gasped.

'And the wooden implement? Where was that?'

The camera turned back to her and she dropped her eyes. 'Inside me,' she whispered.

'Where?'

'In my cunt,' she said harshly.

'And did you like it?'

She nodded instinctively. 'Yes, I... yes.'

'And did you have an orgasm?'

'Yes,' she replied instantly, without having to think about it.

The image on the monitor widened so that her breasts came into the picture, then the entirety of her, from head to knees. She watched the camera zoom in a little and saw the base of the dildo protruding down a little between her thighs.

'Do you want to be used now?' he asked.

'Yes,' she whispered, the erotic tension making her voice crack a little.

'Then beg for it.'

Gwen closed her eyes, her mind spinning. She thought of who he might show the video to, of the dangers of letting such a thing exist, and yet her arousal was so powerful that the wickedness of saying things before it was simply too captivating.

'Please fuck me,' she implored. 'Please fuck my cunt!'

He moved around her, holding the camera. 'Position yourself properly,' he ordered. 'Face down, bottom up.'

She fell forward submissively, sighing as her shoulders touched the floor, her head twisting up to stare at the monitor. He was directly behind her, the camera showing her from behind, bottom raised, legs apart, her sex openly displayed. The camera was positioned carefully to one side and she stared, captivated, at the sight of his fingers approaching her unprotected sex, watched as they stroked her wet lips, her bottom writhing back against them. She watched two straighten and push into her, pumping in and out. A moment later a finger began to stroke her clitoris, and still she watched, eyes wide as the monitor showed her in bright, perfect colour.

He produced a dildo, a thick one, and sank it into her. She stared at her clutching sex lips as they were spread apart, watched as more and more of the dildo disappeared into her body. Then he began to pump and her hips rolled and her eyes stared, held by the captivating sight. And then she yelped even as she saw the hand slap down across her buttocks, yelped again as it spanked a second time, then came, crying out, jerking back against the dildo and his slapping hand.

He left the dildo lodged within her and moved back, circling with the camera, zooming in to her glazed eyes and slack jaw, then pulling back to zoom in on her glistening sex. He filmed her from all angles, then put the camera away and closed the cabinet.

He moved back behind her and knelt, then pulled the dildo free. She heard his zipper sliding down and a moment later gasped as he thrust into her. As before, he used her roughly, powerfully, her bottom aching as his groin slammed against it, her insides punched rhythmically by his pistoning organ as he stabbed into her with all his fury. Yet she knelt and accepted it, unprotesting, gasping and groaning and grunting as he rode her.

And then he finished and rose, and still she knelt there, bottom raised.

'Slut,' he spat.

And she was. She felt both shamed and empowered. Then he gripped her by the arm and dragged her upright to her knees. He held her biceps with both hands, staring down at her without expression. It was impossible to know what was going on in his mind, and she felt anxious and wary again.

Then he unbuckled the restraints and removed them. 'Come with me,' he said.

Chapter 5

Having watched her shower and freshen up he eased a new dildo into her sex, with an attitude of detachment that Gwen found strange, and led her down the hall to the entrance area where the lift was. 'We're going out,' he said, and Gwen stared at him in astonishment as he fetched her coat and shoes from a closet. He held it out and she slipped into it automatically, and then stepped into her shoes.

'Where are we going, sir?' she asked with trepidation.

'To get you properly fitted,' he replied mysteriously as the lift doors whispered open and he guided her inside.

'Fitted, sir?' she probed, though not really sure she wanted to hear the answer.

'Just a few things,' he said noncommittally. 'They need to be sized exactly.'

She nodded as if she understood and then sighed softly; each time she moved the pressure of her thighs against the base of the dildo made a little whisper of pleasure sweep through her.

'Are you going to be obedient?' he asked.

She nodded. 'Yes, sir, I will be obedient.'

He reached out and cupped her face, lifting none too gently. She grabbed at his wrist at first, but at a scowl from him dropped her hands, standing unsteadily on her toes.

'Yes, I think servile obedience is your natural state,' he said, nodding sagely.

Gwendolyn felt indignant but kept silent. He released her chin as the lift stopped and she blushed as the same chauffeur as before stood by the car. She was all too aware of her nudity inside the coat, and averted her eyes as she passed him and climbed into the back of the Cadillac. She sat down gingerly, her bottom sore from her strapping, the dildo still protruding from her pussy.

She felt additional pressure inside her as the round base pushed down against the soft seat, and she winced a little.

He climbed in beside her. 'Are you embarrassed that Paul saw you as a naked whore the other day?' he asked.

She nodded weakly.

'Yes sir!' he snapped.

'Yes sir,' she blurted, jumping a little at the sudden ferocity of the rebuke.

'Well, you shouldn't be.' His voice was instantly soothing again. 'You should be proud of being a whore, and proud of your naked body. You should want to display it to as many men as possible.'

Gwen made an effort to smile, but said nothing.

'Open your coat,' he ordered.

Her heart gave a lurch and she stared at him. 'Now?' she whispered.

'Now,' he confirmed. 'Open it wide.'

'But, sir—'

'Now, slut,' he ordered, the angry tone returning.

She didn't have to, she told herself. She should tell him to stuff it. But the idea, even while hideously embarrassing, was also darkly exciting, and she was slowly undoing the buttons even while her mind was screaming against it. The last button came free, and she opened her coat a few inches, face reddening, but he tugged it wide open, baring her completely.

'Now spread your legs,' he told her.

She felt the words hit her like a blow and could not obey, but his demanding hands gripped her thighs, the fingers like iron, and pried them apart, pulling her bottom forward on the seat so she slumped back a little, making the base of the dildo all too visible.

'Get used to being seen naked,' he hissed venomously, his moods seemingly ever-changing, unsettling her. 'Paul won't be the last man I show you to.'

Gwen stared out of the window, seeing nothing, face burning, stomach churning, glad the window was tinted to hide her nakedness from the traffic around them. Then she heard a whir and turned to see the glass divider between front and rear gliding down.

'Paul, this is Gwendolyn,' Richardson said, as though introducing them at any normal gathering.

'How do you do, Miss Gwendolyn?' Paul said, his eyes grinning at her in the mirror. Gwen gasped and indignantly turned her eyes away.

'Gwendolyn,' Richardson said dangerously, so she turned her gaze back to the mirror, trembling slightly.

'H-hello, Paul,' she managed.

'What do you think of Gwendolyn's body, Paul?'

'Very nice, sir,' the chauffeur said, without elaborating.

'Her breasts?' Richardson cupped one, casually lifting it for his employee.

'Very nice, sir,' Paul said again.

He wanted her; of that Gwen had no doubt. She could see the desire in his dark brown eyes, and a shudder mixing lust and shame churned through her and she had to turn her gaze away again.

She was in a daze as they moved through the traffic, body and mind flustered and confused. Cars drove past them on both sides and people rushed along the pavement. None could see through the tinted glass windows, but she still felt horribly exposed to the world. She flinched as Richardson's cold hand slid between her thighs and he began to rub her clitoris. She shuddered and tried to control herself, determined not to orgasm in front of the chauffeur again.

They turned into a narrow alley and pulled up before a black door. Gwen quickly closed her coat as Richardson got out, scurrying after him, trying not to look at Paul. The door opened before they could reach it and a short man in a black suit welcomed them inside.

'Good afternoon, Mr Richardson,' he gushed. 'It's good to see you again.'

'Thank you, William.' Richardson went through the niceties with little sincerity. 'Is everything ready?'

The plump little sycophant nodded. 'Everything is ready, sir.'

He led them along a narrow, dingy hall, smelling vaguely of old leather and sawdust, then down a flight of steps to a musty, cluttered room.

'The boots first,' Richardson decreed.

'Of course, sir,' William acknowledged with a subservient nod, led Gwen to a chair, then pulled a low stool in front of her as she sat.

'Your foot please, miss,' the little creep said. Gwen swallowed nervously, but raised a foot, quite aware of her nudity beneath the coat and wondering if Richardson would show her to this horrible little man, too.

He measured her feet quite carefully, then her ankles as well. 'Stand up please, miss,' he said when satisfied, and when she did as asked he indicated the coat. 'If you'll now open that, please.'

Gwen stared at Richardson in mute appeal, but he merely nodded.

'But I... I don't have anything on underneath,' she blurted, testing his patience by stating the obvious.

'Mr Kenton has seen naked young women before,' Richardson replied.

Reddening again she opened her coat a little, hesitating, but Richardson grabbed it from behind and roughly snatched it off, leaving her naked before them.

Gwen cringed as Kenton examined her, his beady eyes crawling over her flesh. She felt like dying, like falling through the floor and curling up into a ball. She could hardly breathe for the humiliation.

But, despite the availability of her beauty the man simply got to work, using a tape to measure her legs. She was required to stand still, feet slightly apart, as he knelt before her and ran the tape up the inside of first one leg, and then the other, his fingers almost brushing her bare sex, and the back of a hand actually did briefly touch the base of the dildo. She was fighting to control her breathing, for despite the humiliation she was feeling a deep and growing sexual desire at being so exposed before the seedy little man. A flush spread to her cheeks as he worked methodically; standing to roll the tape around her breasts, directly over her erect nipples to take her bust size.

When he was done, even taking measurements of her head, she was permitted to put the coat back on and do it up.

'All right, sir,' he finally said. 'It'll take a day or two, of course.'

'Of course,' Richardson acknowledged. 'You have the address.'

'Oh yes, sir,' Kenton said, chuckling. 'I have the address.'

Richardson nodded, and motioned a confused but relieved Gwen towards the steps.

They were not done for the day, however. Their next stop was a lingerie store of sorts. They were the only customers and the proprietress, a grey-haired woman, treated Richardson like a king.

Again Gwen had to strip, the dildo still shockingly in place. The woman and Richardson looked at a variety of items, trying the ones he liked on her as though she were a tailor's dummy. The woman never spoke to her, and had no hesitation in adjusting her breasts inside the cups of the bras, or testing the tightness of the strings on thongs, panties or G-strings.

The items he selected would be delivered.

Their next stop was a dress shop. Once again they received private, personal attention, this time from two women, one a few years older than Gwen, the other in her mid-thirties. Once again Gwen had to remove the coat, and this time the younger woman seemed slightly embarrassed and tried not to look at her.

The dresses he bought were all designed to display a woman as provocatively as possible, a few just barely shy of indecent, and that was assuming one was elastic about one's standards.

The younger woman continued to appear slightly flustered by the whole experience, which kept Gwendolyn embarrassed as well. And worse still, after a time Gwen realised the shy blonde was looking at her in a very particular way. That deepened her embarrassment. She had been propositioned by a number of females in the past, but always rebuffed their attentions. It wasn't that the idea especially repulsed her, so much as she was honestly uncertain about just how things would work with a girl. She had no idea how to treat a female lover, and was used to the men taking the lead in things. It was all too confusing, so she'd been quite happy to stick with men.

But now this female was obviously finding her presence deeply arousing.

'Try this,' the older woman said. It was little more than a slip dress, silky and light as a feather. The blonde held it for Gwen, who put her arms out and then raised them as the blonde slid the featherlike material down her arms and over her breasts. One hand brushed against a straining nipple as she pulled it down and Gwen experienced a little static charge of sexual energy.

The white silk was quite tight over her breasts and hips, and fell to just below her buttocks.

'Yes, I like it,' Richardson said. 'What about that slip we saw for around the house?'

'Andrea, fetch it,' the older woman ordered curtly.

The blonde moved away quickly, returning with a small box containing a gold

44

chain and what appeared to be a large scarf. She set it aside and then reached down for the hem of the slip dress, sliding it up. Her fingers gently stroked Gwen's thighs and hips, and then her ribs to brush against the sides of her breasts. Gwen did not respond, raising her arms obediently as the blonde pulled it off.

She gave Gwen a smouldering look before turning and lifting the scarf out of the box. It was too large to be a scarf, Gwen realised, and it had a hole in the centre.

The blonde placed the hole over Gwen's head and let the material fall down her front and back. It was of black silk, and like the slip dress fell to just below her buttocks, but it was completely open on either side and hung freely. The blonde placed the golden chain around her waist then, tightening it so as to draw in the material. Now it was even shorter, exposing the bottom curve of Gwen's buttocks.

'You see that her body is available now without difficulty,' the older woman said, smiling at Richardson. 'You need only ease it aside. Also, you will note the small rings set into the belt. If you wish her restrained you need only clip her wrists to it.'

The blonde, standing to one side, ran her tongue slowly along her lower lip.

Richardson looked pleased. 'All right,' he said. 'We'll take a few of these. Give me six in various colours.'

'Of course, sir,' the woman said obsequiously, bowing a little, then she went with him to the counter to sum up the purchases while the blonde undid the chain, placing it carefully into the box. She reached for the hem of the shift and a finger trailed between Gwen's thighs, then eased a little higher. Gwen started as she felt the finger trace a line against her straining pussy lips, circling the base of the dildo, and stared at the girl, who smiled, a finger gently pushing up against the base of the dildo.

'D-don't,' Gwen whispered, but the mischievous blonde held the dildo and eased several inches out. She looked down, and Gwen instinctively did the same, seeing the black plastic glistening with her juices in the overhead light.

'You like cocks?' the girl whispered, then pushed the dildo up, letting her thump stroke across Gwen's clitoris. Her other hand moved up and cupped one of her breasts, squeezing fully as she leaned in and nibbled the nape of her neck. Gwen's heart began to pound and she shuddered as the dildo began to ease in and out. She was in such a state of tense arousal that her hips started to grind instinctively and she gripped the blonde's shoulders, gasping for breath.

Then the blonde pulled back, quickly lifting the flimsy garment off her and turning away as she folded it and put it into the box. Gwen was left on trembling legs, trying to catch her breath.

Richardson and the older woman returned, the woman holding a skirt, a white blouse and a blazer, as well as a pair of flat shoes. Gwen looked at them in surprise, wondering why the total contrast in style compared to what she had spent the day modelling.

'That will do very nicely,' Richardson said.

Gwen was grateful to put her own coat on once more. They returned to the car and Paul drove them back towards the penthouse while she tried to calm her conflicting emotions. This, of course, was a forlorn task, as Richardson almost immediately opened her coat once more to display her body to Paul.

'The naked female form is an object of veneration and worship,' he said. 'You should be proud of your fine breasts, your soft skin, your sculpted hips and legs.'

'But I'm not used to being naked around strangers,' she protested weakly.

'Many men have seen you naked, have they not?' he goaded.

'Not *many*,' she objected. 'I've had lovers but, well, that's different. What you're making me do is so... so strange.'

'It won't seem strange soon.'

She looked at him curiously. 'And what was the last outfit for?' she asked. 'The skirt and blazer.'

'You wondered, did you?' he mused.

She nodded.

'It's a present for your father,' he said. 'When you go back to him that's the way you'll be dressing. I thought I'd buy your first outfit.'

Gwen pouted, then looked down at her nudity. 'I wouldn't be caught dead in an outfit like that,' she muttered.

'You'll be an obedient girl, just as you're now my obedient little slut,' he stated firmly, and then turned to the driver. 'Paul, stop here,' he ordered.

The limousine pulled over to the kerb and Gwen looked at Richardson uncertainly. He opened the door and got out, then held his arm in for her. She closed her coat and climbed out beside him, just outside the garage entrance to his apartment building. He smiled and reached for the buttons of her coat.

'Please, I'll be arrested,' she gasped.

He chuckled. 'Nonsense.' Gwen tried to hold the coat tightly but he forced it open, then pushed it back over her shoulders, pulled it off, and tossed it into the back of the car. Then he slammed the door and the Cadillac pulled away.

The street was brightly lit and the traffic was almost continuous in both directions. She froze, gripped by shock, her mind in turmoil as Richardson took her wrist and turned her to face the passing vehicles. 'We won't go in until you straighten up and put your arms down,' he said sternly.

'Please,' she begged, utterly mortified, the cold biting into her flesh.

'Sir.'

'Please, sir!'

'If you prolong this through disobedience the police may well turn up, and then just imagine the adverse publicity you'll get. I'll be gone before they get here, but you'll have to face the consequences of your stubbornness.'

Gwen knew it was hopeless and stopped resisting, her heart pounding and face scarlet as she dropped her hands to her sides and stood with a straight back, watching the traffic flood past, doing anything to end the ordeal quickly. She was naked on a busy street corner in the middle of New York City. Nothing had ever prepared her for anything remotely similar to such a trial. It was cold, but her goosebumps had little to do with the temperature. She could see faces staring at her, could see shock and amazement as they stared.

At last Richardson took her hand then slowly turned her and walked into the garage. Thankfully it was deserted. His key opened the inner gate, and they were soon in the warm lift and on the way up to the relative sanctuary of his apartment.

'Interesting experience?' he asked lightly. 'You'll have to learn that obedience is the first rule for every servant,' he went on. 'I don't want you continually questioning my orders and trying to resist them.'

'I - I'm sorry, sir,' she whispered, feeling genuinely humbled.

'You lack discipline,' he said. 'You need to learn it quickly.'

Gwen nodded, her mind still frozen with the shocked embarrassment and strange excitement of being naked on a busy street. He held her hand as they exited the lift and headed along the hall. She knew where they were going, and felt a new stirring of excitement mixed with alarm. She could, of course, simply refuse whatever he intended, and comforted herself with that thought even as they entered the room and her eyes were caught by the chains dangling overhead.

He placed two thick leather restraints around her wrists, and then clipped them together behind her back by means of the simple rings that adorned them. 'Here,' he ordered.

It was an A-shaped steel frame with a roll of padding over the middle crossbar. Richardson pressed her against it, spreading her legs until they were against the frame's legs, then strapping them tightly in place at ankles, knees and thighs, and being so tightly, irrevocably bound was causing her insides to flutter and stir.

He pushed on her back and she bent forward across the padded crossbar, feeling it press into her lower belly. She felt utterly exposed to him, and this increased her sensation of wickedness.

He pushed her down until she was bent right forward, and then she was surprised to feel his fingers combing her hair back and gathering it together at the top of her head. He wound it in a long loose braid, and then tugged it upwards, forcing her to lift her head until she was looking forward. Somehow he tied her long tresses up, probably to the top of the A-frame. She could not turn her head to look due to the pull. Still, she did not protest. A dark hunger was growing inside her, and she knew she was already wet. Her stomach was fluttering and her chest was tight with anxiety as she wondered what he would do to her, but neither could affect the already intense arousal blurring her thoughts.

'Ow...' she squealed as a clip was snapped onto her erect left nipple, and she winced and moaned as she waited for her body to get used to the sensation. A moment later a second clip joined it on her other nipple. She could not look down, but as he snapped whatever the clips were attached to in place she failed to sense the kind of swinging she had felt with the weights he used before. Instead she felt a solid hold.

She tried to straighten up a little and her nipples ached much more harshly.

She was breathless with anticipation, anxious despite her arousal, yet determined to take whatever punishment he delivered.

A low buzzing sound startled her and for a moment raised her anxieties, then she felt the push of something hard against her sex, and the vibrations that ran through her body immediately told her what it was. She had never felt a vibrator, and for long moments her arousal and unease were set aside as she attempted to analyse the sensations. At first the vibrations were actually mildly unpleasant, too severe, too strong as he ran the thing near her clitoris. As he continued, however, her sex began to throb in sympathy with the device, and her clitoris in particular began to thrum with delight. She found her breathing growing faster and faster, her insides heaving as her belly glowed with warmth. And then she groaned. He had, without warning, penetrated her with the device; thrust it firmly in one smooth stroke deep into her body.

The thing was long enough that the buzzing tip rested almost against her cervix, and her entire body was trembling lightly in tandem to its powerful vibrations. He moved alongside her, reaching down to give one of her breasts a squeeze that sent an aching heat flooding up into her chest. Then he lifted a small mirror onto a table and placed the table just to the right of her head, angling it to catch the wall across from her. A moment later he positioned the large mirror she had watched herself in that very morning, placing it so that it caught her from the side, in profile.

She shuddered to see herself, a deep aching throb echoing up from her groin, through her belly and up to her chest. Then she saw him holding a long leather belt in one hand, raising his arm in the air. She watched it, dazed; watched his arm draw back further, and then whip forward. In the mirror the belt swung through the air and landed directly across her upraised bottom.

Crack!

She cried out at the sharp lash of pain that snapped through her. Her body jerked against the powerful bonds holding her legs in place, and she felt the tight pressure of the straps digging into her flesh, especially those locked tightly around her thighs.

Again he brought the belt down and again she cried out, her vaginal muscles squeezing powerfully around the vibrator inside her, and she felt a sharp tug on her hair as her head jerked forward.

Crack! Crack! Crack! Crack!

The pain began to mount, and she knew a moment of near panic as her buttocks began to heat, then a flood of wicked desire threw the pain back, or joined with it to make the two sensations one. The strap landed again and she felt a small explosion of joy deep in her trembling groin. Another blow landed, and another, as she moaned and gasped and squeezed her muscles around the vibrator.

Through blurred eyes she saw him stop, go to the wall and replace the strap, then take down a long thin riding crop and move once more into position behind her.

She groaned aloud, and then clenched her jaws as the crop cut down. It made a swishing sound as it cut through the air, then bit into her flank with a painful stab that made her cry out once more.

The pain mounted and sweat coated her body, making her skin glisten in the golden light filling the room. Her eyes were filled with tears as another blow landed, and then another. Fire gripped her bottom, burning through her body and mind as more blows landed. And yet even through the pain the pleasure continued to grow, continued to spread its grip upon her.

She saw him turn the crop, sliding it between her tightly bound thighs. She felt it caress her skin, then snap upwards. The tip caught her clitoris, making her scream, and then he slid it back roughly so it clawed along her furrow. Immediately he thrust it forward again, sawing the edge of it back and forth along her naked slit, grinding the tip across her engorged clitoris with merciless force.

The pleasure and pain wound together once more, twisting and spiralling until she thought she would scream. The climax exploded and she cried out, shuddering and pulling at her bonds, her bottom instinctively trying to thrust back as her pleasure soared.

Her pussy spasmed around the invading vibrator, and her breasts ached as her jerking body pulled against the clamps locked to them. The sensations assaulted her from all directions and she gurgled mindlessly, the air escaping her lungs as she trembled and shook.

Gwen came out of it slowly. She raised her head weakly and groaned as his body blocked her view. He had undressed, and his erection was inches from her face, but she barely had time to note it before he pushed forward and thrust into her mouth. She sucked instinctively, and then began to caress the underside of the head with her tongue. Her bottom hurt but she focused her attention on his cock as he pumped possessively in and out. Her cheeks drew inward as she applied herself and he began to thrust with deeper strokes, using her mouth as he did her pussy.

He reached down and squeezed her breasts. Then he chuckled and his hands moved along her back, caressing the soft skin and then cupping her bottom. She felt a new surge of pain as his hands traced the welts of her beating. One hand moved away, the other stroked directly between the cleft of her buttocks, lightly fingering her anal opening. She felt his finger slowly pushing into her and mumbled a protest around his pumping cock. The finger eased deeper, exploring as it slowly squirmed and sank into her.

'Have you ever been fucked in the ass?' he asked casually.

Shock tightened her chest as his crude words sank into her mind. She never had, fearing it would hurt, or at least be particularly unpleasant and somewhat degrading. The very notion had always repulsed her. She simply could not let him do that.

And yet her feelings, she realised, were something of a reflex. If she let him bugger her it would certainly not influence his opinions of her; she was a mere sexual toy to him anyway - nothing more.

He pulled out of her mouth and rubbed the wet head of his organ back and forth over her face. 'Have you ever been fucked in the ass?' he demanded again, his abrupt crudity hitting her like a physical slap.

'N-no, sir,' she gasped, her voice quavering.

'Think you're too good for it, do you?' he sneered.

'Yes, sir,' she admitted without thinking.

His finger continued to twist within her bottom, and he added a second as he pushed his hips forward once more. She took him into her mouth again, gagging slightly as he pushed deep.

'There are so many things for you to learn, my little English slut,' he mused, then pulled out and moved behind her and removed the vibrator. She groaned as he began to roll the slick head along her furrow and over her clitoris, and then she stiffened as she felt something other than a finger pressing against her anus.

'No... don't... not *there*...' she moaned, and then slumped in her bonds as she gazed mistily at her image in the mirror and shuddered at the sight of his gnarled cock spearing from the dark shadows of his groin, sinking slowly, inexorably, into that very private passage.

The head forced past her tight ring of muscle with more ease than she imagined it would, and he began to pump gently in and out, easing it deeper and deeper as his hands clamped her hips.

'*Please*,' she gasped.

He covered her back and squeezed her breasts possessively, his fingers tugging at the nipple clamps, cruelly tormenting the distended buds.

'Ooohhh...' she groaned as he pushed particularly deep, her head spinning with conflicting emotions. He was using her steadily, dispassionately, pleasing himself without thought for her. She could feel his testicles slapping against her tender sex lips as he drove fully into her each time, and the coarse hairs of his groin and lower belly as he ground against her sore buttocks.

'Lovely and tight,' he grunted hoarsely, his excitement evident. He picked up speed, and then abruptly gave several furious thrusts and came inside her. She sighed, partly with relief, partly with disappointment, and he pulled slowly back and out.

Chapter 6

The vibrator was still buried inside her, and the sight of her bound to the apparatus continued to arouse as she looked into the mirror. Her anus felt empty and her buttocks flamed. Her pussy was on fire as well, and she worked her muscles weakly against the buzzing sex toy as she waited for him to return.

He was away for some time and her frustration mounted. She could not quite bring herself off as she was. But the vibrator and her own bound position kept her in a state of arousal. Her head was starting to ache too, for having it raised for so long was extremely tiring, and she had for some time been forced to let at least some of the weight be held by her bound hair.

Gwen heard his footsteps at last, and winced as she tried to turn her head to see him.

'Getting bored without me, slut?' he asked.

'No, sir,' she said weakly.

'Oh? Perhaps you want more time to reflect on things?'

'No, sir,' she protested, 'that's not what I meant.'

He untied her hair and her head fell heavily, her hair spilling around her face. Then he released her legs, one strap at a time, and finally he removed the vibrator and freed her wrists.

She swayed unsteadily as he pulled her upright and supported her until feeling returned to her legs. He then turned her and pulled her wrists back behind her, clipping the restraints in place there. A collar slipped around her throat and a leash was snapped to the front. Then he led her out of the room and back along the hall to one of the smaller sitting rooms. He knelt her before a large leather armchair and ordered her to sit back on her heels and spread her knees wide before sitting in front of her.

There was a large gas fire to one side, and the flick of a switch on a little remote control device sent tall flames licking and dancing in the grate. He picked up a glass of brandy from the table on his other side and sipped as he examined her. 'Keep your back straight,' he ordered sharply.

'Yes, sir, Mr Richardson,' she said.

'Sir will do. I did not give you permission to use my name.'

'I'm sorry, sir.'

'What should I do with you, slut girl?' he said acidly.

'I don't know, sir.'

He pondered for a while, swilling the amber liquid around in the glass. 'Tell me about Gwendolyn Allison Pepperdine,' he said eventually.

'Sir?' She wasn't at all sure what he wanted to know.

'Tell me about her family,' he qualified.

'I don't really have much of one.'

'Sir!' he snapped, making her flinch from his sudden ferocity.

'S-sorry, sir,' she blurted hastily.

'Father?'

'Stepfather,' she confirmed. 'My father died when I was a baby and my mother married his cousin shortly afterwards. *Lord* Pepperdine,' she stressed sarcastically. 'He considers himself a great thinker and humanitarian.'

'He's a politician?'

'Good heavens no,' she snorted. 'Him stand for election? He'd never do something so common.' She shifted her sore buttocks on her heels and then hurriedly added, 'Sir,' as he glared.

'So how did he get his money? Inheritance?'

'He wasted his on something or other. Father had a lot though, and mother inherited that. He *manages* it,' she said sourly. 'My mother's parents must have hated him. When they died it turned out they'd left her nothing because they knew he'd get control of it. Instead they left all their money to me in a trust for when I turn twenty-one.'

'Ah, I see,' he said, nodding as he absorbed her words. 'But until then you're under the old man's thumb.'

She made a face of displeasure. 'Yes sir, I am.'

'And he wants his stepdaughter to show a little respect.'

'Yes sir, that's about it,' she confirmed.

'So do you think he liked that picture of you in the tabloids?' he asked, and Gwen blushed slightly at the thought of it. 'Perhaps you could pose for a real men's magazine. What do you think? That would surely annoy him.'

'I - I don't think that would be a good idea, sir,' she said uncertainly, wondering what he was getting at.

'I bet you'd like to pose for such pictures,' he mused, idly running a fingertip around the rim of his glass, golden reflections of the fire dancing in the crystal. 'I bet you'd come just from seeing them.'

Gwen shifted uncomfortably on her heels again.

'Imagine how angry he'd be,' he went on, a calculating smile playing across his lips. 'Gwendolyn,' his voice spoke her name in rich deep tones, 'I want you to write something for me.'

He leaned over her and unsnapped the wrist restraints, then placed a paper and pen on the table.

'What, sir?' she asked, puzzled.

'I will dictate and you will write,' he told her.

She leaned forward uncertainly, wondering what he was up to, her bare breasts pressing against the edge of the low table, the nipple weights making small clacking sounds as they touched the wood.

'Dear father,' he said. She hesitated, and then wrote the words. 'I had a wonderful time today. I had sex with ten different men.' Gwen frowned, but continued anyway. 'I walked down the street wearing only my short coat, and opened it to every attractive man I saw, offering them sex with me.' She wrote, her eyes flitting up at him in confusion. 'I find I am happy only when being fucked, and have come to the conclusion that I want nothing in life but to be a whore.'

The pen hovered and Gwen looked at him fully. 'I'm not going to sign this,' she stated firmly.

'I am beginning to enjoy being buggered, too,' he went on, paying her no attention, gazing at the brandy with amusement in his eyes.

'Why am I writing this?' she asked in exasperation.

'For the same reason you do anything: because I told you to,' he said casually, and then went on, 'I've heard that successful prostitutes can have sex with many men in one day, and I envy them.' Gwen dutifully wrote the words, thinking the man slightly insane. 'I don't want any of your money, nor even the money from my trust. I want only to be a prostitute, to be used again and again by man after man, all day and all night.'

Gwen couldn't believe the nonsense he was making her write. Oh well, she thought, if it pleased him.

'Now sign it,' he commanded, and she looked up uncertainly. 'Sign it.'

'I won't have this sent to him,' she said defiantly.

He sipped his brandy and then smiled lazily. 'Why?'

'Because he...'

'Because you don't want him to know what a whore you really are?' he stated for her.

Gwen wavered, not knowing what to say.

'You do realise that no one will believe it's for real? They'll simply imagine you wrote it to antagonise your stepfather.'

Well, she supposed that was true. She was known for possessing an odd sense of humour.

'Now come along, Gwendolyn,' he said with exaggerated patience, 'be a good girl and sign it.'

She stared at him, then down at the letter, and feeling she had no will of her own, she signed her name, feeling strangely detached as she did so. He leaned forward and slid it off the table, then read as she knelt anxiously, wondering what his intentions were. Then he smiled, and tore it into a number of small pieces.

'Sometimes it's good for us to write, just to see our thoughts with our own eyes.'

He motioned her forward, then turned her and locked her restraints behind her back once more before turning her back. 'Do your friends know what a whore you are?' he mocked.

'I don't think anyone knows what a... a whore I am, sir,' she said quietly. 'I'm not sure I knew myself until, well...'

'Until I showed you.' He stretched out a leg, his foot pressing up against her pussy, rubbing lightly.

'Yes, sir,' she confirmed.

'Do you have a best friend?' he asked.

'Yes, sir; Candice.'

'And what do you suppose she'd think if she knew what you'd been doing recently?'

'I suppose she'd think I was an incredible slut, sir.'

'Maybe we could send her that videotape,' he chuckled. 'Do you like that idea, Gwendolyn?'

'No, sir,' she said. 'I don't.'

He smiled and sipped his drink, then set the crystal glass down and leaned forward and removed the nipple clips, before sitting back, watching her expression of anguish as the surge of returning feelings made her pull frantically against the restraints binding her wrists. He continued pressing the toe of his shoe against her sex, rubbing slowly against her.

'I adore your nipples,' he stated evenly. 'They look so delicate, so vulnerable.'

'Yes, sir,' she managed, despite the storm of discomfort raging in her breasts, despite her yearning to cup and comfort them; a yearning heightened by her inability to do so. And then she realised she was slowly grinding her hips, rubbing her sex against the toe of his shoe. The realisation shocked her, but at the same time aroused her. She didn't know why it should, but it seemed that each new depth to which he lowered her induced a higher level of sexual abandon.

'Would you like me to fuck you now, Gwendolyn?' he suddenly asked bluntly.

She couldn't deny that she would like that, very much. 'Yes, sir,' she sighed.

'Beg me.'

'Please fuck me, sir,' she panted.

He sipped his brandy again and then chuckled. 'No,' he said, 'I don't think so. I think you're doing well enough there on my foot. Have you ever masturbated on someone's foot before, Gwendolyn Allison Pepperdine?'

'No,' she gasped, her face reddening further.

'Are you close to coming?' he asked.

'I... I... yes,' she gasped, but he withdrew his foot and her hips slowly stopped grinding as she looked up at him forlornly. He got up and moved behind her, then knelt. She gasped as a hand yanked back on her hair, then his teeth were chewing lightly the nape of her neck as his free hand cupped her breasts. He pinched her nipples then slid his hand down between her legs, and she shuddered as his fingers pressed against her clitoris and began to rub. At once her hips began to rock once more, driving herself against them.

'Do you want to come?' he demanded, hissing in her ear.

'Oh yes, sir...' she wailed.

'Are you nearly there?'

'Yes, sir... I am.'

He stood, pulling her up then dispassionately shunting her forward so she stumbled. Then he pushed her against his armchair so the padded leather arm was between her thighs, her left leg bent with her knee and shin on the cushion, her right leg straight and supporting most of her weight.

'Then come,' he commanded. 'Right now; let me see you come.'

Gwen felt the pressure of the arm up against her moist sex, and a new wave of humiliation swept over her even as she began to grind against it. He stepped back, watching intently, and she rocked her hips with increasing fervour, feeling the cool leather pressing up into her sex, gasping as it became slick and rubbed against her. Her breasts were moulding against the edge of the chair's back and she rolled against it, the awareness of how she was degrading herself like daggers in her mind as she gasped in helpless need.

The climax began as a sharp explosion between her legs, and then flared up and out. She shuddered as she frantically worked her body against the chair, crying out in short gasps each time a new bolt of wondrous pleasure lashed her body. For long seconds she rode the solid piece of furniture, and then collapsed across it, her breasts heaving as she breathed deeply, feeling intensely embarrassed.

He gave her a moment to recover, then pulled her off the chair and held her from behind, examining the glistening wetness along the leather arm. 'Is that how you behave at your stepfather's house?' he asked cruelly, intentionally bringing attention to her shame. Then without awaiting an answer he chuckled and led her from the room.

Gwen stumbled along at the end of her leash, trying to understand why she was so excited about demeaning herself so utterly before him.

They returned to the dungeon room, where her replaced her leather restraints with thin gold shackles. This time he let her have her wrists in front of her, but ran a chain between the new gold collar around her throat down through the linked shackles around her wrists, to the chain linking the two on her ankles. She could not raise her hands very high, nor lower them very far, and she especially could not touch herself between the legs.

Then she was forced to shuffle as he led her back, taking small steps while he guided her to the kitchen. 'You have two choices, girl,' he said. 'You can make me dinner, or clean the floor. Which will it be?'

Gwen was not much of a cook, but that was better than cleaning a floor - something she had never done, of course, nor had any wish to do. 'I'll make your dinner, sir,' she said.

'Then it had better be good,' he stated severely. 'And if I don't like it you'll be punished.'

He disappeared, probably, she thought, to his little theatre, as she soon heard the distant sound of a television.

Most of the food was fairly simple, consisting of meat in the freezer, microwave dinners and cans of soup and stew. Could she get away with stuffing something into the microwave? Possibly, but she thought it likely he was testing her in some way. He would want her to cook something substantial. She could do a steak; that would impress him.

As she busied herself, Gwen gave little thought as to why she wanted to impress him.

Getting the ingredients was a challenge in itself. She could not raise her shackled wrists as high as her breasts, and had to carry over a stool and carefully climb it before being able to even remove the steaks from the freezer. Getting other items was a similar problem, but she managed to cope - just. She found a cookbook as well, and then dug out some pots and pans.

Every few minutes as she tried to cook dinner she experienced a little shiver of excitement at being shackled and naked. It was quite bizarre in many ways but certainly more exciting than any other effort at cooking she could recall.

She felt perversely domesticated as she set the table, then finished the steaks and tipped the chopped mushrooms beside them on their plates, then placed the two plates on the table, knowing as she did that she was being presumptuous. Still, he hadn't told her not to make something for herself. Then she shuffled quickly down the hall and stopped at the door to the theatre. 'Excuse me, sir, dinner is ready,' she announced.

He followed her back to the dining room, looked at the two steaks, then at her. Gwen blushed. 'I don't recall inviting you to eat,' he said coldly.

'Oh, I'm sorry, sir,' she replied disappointedly, feeling really very hungry.

He sat down and picked up a knife and fork, then cut into the steak and ate. He chewed carefully as he studied her, and then nodded slowly. 'Very good,' he said approvingly. 'Well done.'

Gwen felt a wave of relief and delight - and then annoyance that she should be reduced to feeling either having just cooked a meal for some arrogant man she barely knew.

'Because of that I'll let you eat, as well,' he decreed.

'Thank you, sir,' she said, reaching for the nearest chair.

'Not at the table, of course,' he added, raising a hand to stop her, and then he picked up her plate and put it on the floor beside his chair, and it was obvious he had no intention of placing the knife and fork with it. 'As befits a slut,' he mused.

'Yes, sir,' she said, feeling a little hurt after the effort she'd gone to for him; few men had enjoyed the luxury of having Gwendolyn Allison Pepperdine cook for them!

But she crouched down on her knees and shackled hands, and set about trying to eat the steak without the benefit of knife or fork. It was awkward and messy, but at the same time the sheer humility she experienced was oddly arousing.

After dinner and after stacking the dishwasher Gwen was allowed to kneel beside his armchair as he relaxed and watched a movie, and after a time she was ordered to fellate him. For reasons she herself did not properly understand she chose to antagonise him by using her teeth to continually nip him, not to hurt but to goad, until she got the reaction she'd deep down been longing for, and he grabbed her by the hair and dragged her to the dungeon.

But instead of punishing her, or perhaps as a punishment, he stood her in the centre of the room and chained her arms above her head and spread apart.

This both aroused and frightened her, thinking he was about to hang her by her wrists and whip her. But all he did was spread her legs, shackle her ankles down, and leave her as she was.

All night.

With the heavy door closed shouting, cursing and begging were pointless. All Gwen could do was wait for him to return and free her. It was an excruciatingly long night and her legs and arms grew painfully stiff, cramped and sore long before morning, hence she was deeply relieved when the door finally opened and Richardson appeared, already immaculately dressed for a day's work. She was tired and in a foul mood but, fearing he would leave her as she was all day if she antagonised him further, said nothing.

'Have we learned our lesson?' he asked.

'Yes, sir,' she said, doing a poor job of keeping the resentment out of her voice.

He smiled lightly, pinching one of her nipples as he stood before her. 'I think there's still too much of the brat in you to learn so quickly,' he said, and then undid the shackles holding her and she groaned with undiluted relief as she was finally able to flex her numb limbs.

'The alternative to obedience need not be pain,' he told. 'It might just be boredom,' and with that casual remark he turned and left, and she glared after him.

Gwen sat for long quiet minutes in reflective mood, drawing her knees up to her chin one at a time and luxuriating in the delicious sensation of movement. Finally she rose, not bothering to find clothing, went into the kitchen and made breakfast, then had a long hot bath during which she drifted off to sleep.

After the revitalising bath she dried herself and gratefully spent much of the day dozing on the sofa in the lounge or sleeping on his huge bed.

A warbling tone woke her and she sat up and rubbed her eyes, looking around the room in confusion for the source of the noise. Then, realising it was coming from outside the bedroom, she got up and made her way along the hall, and gazed doubtfully at the little entrance console next to the lift.

In the monitor she saw a man, and recognised him as Kenton. He stood in the small lobby, a large box on the floor beside him. The sight of the little creep made her shudder, but she knew he was working to Richardson's instructions, and so it would be wise to see what he wanted. She pressed the talk button on the console. 'Yes?' she said into the small grille, watching him look up into the camera.

'I have Mr Richardson's order, miss,' his metallic voice informed her.

Gwen still considered sending the weasel away, but the thought of an angry Richardson dissuaded her from being so rash. So she pressed the button that opened the lower lift doors and watched him shuffle in and then come into view of the second camera set in the lift. Then she hurried into Richardson's bedroom and quickly put on one of his silk robes.

She was back just as the lift doors glided silently open and Kenton shoved the box out and into the hall. 'Here you are,' he said, panting quite heavily and mopping sweat from his large brow with a hanky. Clearly he was not the fittest individual in the world.

'Um, Mr Richardson isn't available at the moment,' Gwen said hesitantly.

'Oh, I know,' Kenton wheezed. 'He said he wouldn't be, but it's only you I need to see, anyway.' Gwen looked at him suspiciously, but he merely went on. 'I'm sure they'll all fit properly but Mr Richardson said you were to try everything on before signing for them.'

He opened the box and first drew out a pair of stiletto shoes. The heel was, she guessed, six inches in height, and she shook her head in amazement as he knelt and buckled them onto her feet without saying another word. They fitted perfectly, but walking in them felt quite bizarre, and she knew she would need more practice before she could move with any grace in heels so high.

Kenton removed them, then turned back to the box and drew out a pair of boots. Gwen had never seen their like; they too had six-inch stiletto heels and looked as though they'd reach the tops of her thighs.

Bill unzipped the right one and held it out for her, and with some difficulty she slipped her foot into it, pushing down until it folded over her ankle and then lower calf. The leather drew up higher, and he opened her robe without any hesitation, seemingly ignoring her nudity as he zipped the boot slowly up past her knee and up her thigh. The top of the boot was tapered, with the inside snug against the flesh of her inner thigh just below her sex, and the outer edge riding up to her hip.

He quickly helped her into the second boot and then stood back. Despite her discomfort at being alone with the creep, Gwen was intrigued by the boots, although more than a little appalled at the idea of trying to walk in them.

'How's the fit?' he asked.

'Um, they seem to fit nicely,' she confirmed, walking slowly and carefully back and forth.

'Excellent,' he beamed. He dug into the box again and came out with a pair of leather gloves. Like the boots, they were long, reaching up to her armpits. She gazed at herself in the mirrored wall before the elevators and felt a thrum of sexual elation at the sight of herself, barely able to keep from sliding a hand down between her legs, even though he was drooling behind her. And then a leather G-string and bra made her feel less naked.

The next item to be drawn from the box shocked her briefly; a T-shaped leather belt, the horizontal strip for her waist and the vertical strip to snake between her thighs and fasten at the back. In the centre of the latter length of leather was a long, thick, leather protrusion - a dildo at least eight or nine inches long.

Kenton held it up with a salacious leer. 'Mr Richardson said you have to try on *everything*, miss,' he slavered. Gwen looked away and considered refusing the instruction, but even after only one day under the control of Richardson her tolerance for such embarrassments had increased significantly.

'Very well, if that's what he wants,' she said. 'But not with you leering at me.' She took the belt into the bedroom and removed the G-string, then examined the thing, feeling a wicked bubble of excitement in the pit of her stomach. She fed it between her legs and slowly pushed the dildo up into her pussy, feeling wildly sluttish as she did. Then she buckled the belt around her waist and drew the vertical strap up at the back, where it buckled together.

With a red face Gwen ran her fingers over the device in awe, and then walked unsteadily back to where Kenton was eagerly waiting in the hall.

'Meant to be tighter,' he said, then unbuckled the rear strap, tugged it up harder, and then fastened it again. Gwen felt the pressure jam up against and into her sex, but did not protest in any way.

Getting on with his task with evident relish, Kenton removed her bra without asking and lifted a sort of halter out of the box. It fitted snugly beneath her breasts, lifting and squeezing them firmly together.

The straps then continued up to fasten behind her neck, and a final strap crossed horizontally over the top of her breasts, pinching them in a form of tight leather bondage.

'Excellent,' he said, running his fingers reverently over the straps.

A leather hood followed and Gwen eyed it doubtfully, but let him fold it over her head without complaint. It had a hole for her mouth, two for her eyes and two smaller ones for her nostrils. Then came a ball-gag, which Kenton gleefully fed into her mouth and fastened at the back of her head, forcing her jaw wide and pinning her tongue down.

By this time Gwen was meekly letting him do whatever he wished, and made no objection when he slipped her fitted leather restraints around her gloved wrists and then linked them together behind her back.

He quickly produced several small locks, attaching them to the buckles holding the gag and belt in place and snapping them closed.

'Mr Richardson said I was to prepare you for his return,' he told her. 'He wants to find you waiting for him in some of your delicious new outfits.'

Kenton fed restraints around her ankles and attached a bar between them to keep her legs apart, then strapped a padded leather blindfold over her eyes. Gwen heard a few sounds after that, but was then shocked when he said goodbye and left her as she was.

She felt extremely aroused, but now also extremely annoyed. Once more she was left tied up with nothing to occupy her spinning mind but nagging discomfort. With no small effort she managed to shuffle back and to the side, to where she knew there was a chair, and, with quite some difficulty, sat down to wait for Richardson's return. She tested the restraints without much optimism, and they proved to be as immoveable as she suspected they would be.

Chapter 7

A short time later the sound of the lift rising pulled Gwen out of the chair and she stood waiting in anticipation for his arrival, but cringed when she heard his voice and realised he was talking to someone else.

'Just put them over there,' he said.

Knowing she was all but naked in front of a stranger was not quite as shocking as it would have been only a day or so before, but the bizarre outfit she wore still had her slowly shaking her head in denial that this could be happening.

'Hey, what a beauty,' a man said from just in front of her, and then she felt fingers at the back of her head and the blindfold was removed, causing her to blink against the sudden light.

There were two people with Richardson. One was the blonde girl from the dress store with several boxes she had just finished setting on the table. She gave Gwen a suggestive look from the corner of her eye.

The other was a man of similar age to his host, well dressed, but nothing much to look at. As Gwen eyed him cautiously Richardson dismissed the blonde and she left, throwing another wistful glance at Gwen as the closing mouth of the lift swallowed her.

'So David, what do you think?' Richardson asked of his companion, seemingly unaware of the silent contact between the two girls.

'I'm extremely jealous,' the newcomer said.

'Think I should keep her like this?' Richardson asked conversationally, as though discussing a new pet.

The newcomer shook his head thoughtfully, his eyes still glued to Gwen. 'Not permanently, although she looks a real treat.'

Richardson bent down and removed the spreader bar. 'Come into the lounge,' he said, waving the man forward and then guiding Gwen by the arm.

'So, what's her name?' the man asked.

'Anne,' Richardson replied, and then introduced them with a formality that belied the outlandishness of the situation. 'Anne, meet David Cotter - David Cotter, meet Anne.'

She turned her eyes on him, glaring, thankful he had maintained her anonymity but wishing he had come up with something more stylish than Anne.

'So, does she obey you in everything?' Cotter asked with lust in his bulging eyes as they ravished her.

'She still requires disciplining from time to time,' Richardson said, sitting back in one of the antique chairs. 'And she does still have a lot to learn.'

'I'll bet,' Cotter replied, his voice thick with lust.

Richardson snapped his fingers at her and she turned as directed, so he could unfasten her restraints. He cupped her bottom for a moment and then slapped it lightly. 'Brandy for Mr Cotter,' he said. 'And I'll have a scotch and soda.'

Gwen obeyed, moving as smoothly as she could in the high heels, then prepared their drinks at the small bar and returned. For some reason feeling the need to play to her role diligently, she knelt before Richardson and bowed her head as she presented his glass, cradling it in her cupped hands.

'Very good, slut,' he said.

She rose, walked the few feet to Cotter, and then eased down onto her knees again, presenting his glass in the same manner. His eyes and mouth were wide and she noticed an evident tenting of his trousers as he took the glass.

She returned to Richardson who locked her wrists behind her back again, then pulled her up to sit astride his lap, where he idly fondled her breasts as Cotter looked on hungrily. 'Yes, it's taken quite of lot of training so far, but she's beginning to learn her place,' he said airily. 'She's already learned to enjoy crawling.'

'How did you find her?' Cotter demanded, the glass trembling slightly in his hand.

'You have to be able to recognise submissiveness in a woman, David, and help her to recognise it as well.'

Gwen watched Cotter closely, basking in his obvious hunger and desire, and then felt Richardson unlocking the belt; and she felt a sudden rush of embarrassment, excitement and daring.

'Spread your legs,' he ordered, and she obeyed, blushing behind the hood, parting her thighs so Cotter would have an unrestricted view as the belt was moved aside and he saw the dildo embedded between her soft, moist lips.

'Hell!' he exclaimed enthusiastically.

Richardson pulled an inch or so out, then slid it back in. His fingers moved up and began to stroke her clitoris, and she rolled her hips in helpless excitement even as her embarrassment grew. 'She's a sexual animal now,' Richardson said.

And that was true. Gwen could feel the sexual heat intensifying between her legs, flooding through her belly and catching her breath in her lungs. She breathed raggedly through the small holes in the hood, grunting into the gag as she spread her thighs wider still.

Her gaze remained locked on Cotter, watching the lust reflected in his eyes and face, the amazement and awe and need etched there. She felt smug arrogance at the way her body was affecting him, at his desperate desire for her. And along with it was a wild sense of freedom at her anonymity. She didn't have to care what he thought of her, or who he told about her. She was a faceless body to him, an unknown object of desire.

She groaned more loudly, wanting to ensure he heard her through the gag, and began to roll her groin more urgently against Richardson's finger. He pumped the dildo in and out for a while and she mewled and writhed against him. Then he resumed fingering her clitoris and she laid her head back on his shoulder, rolling it from side to side as pleasure and excitement swamped her.

She came, writhing on his lap, breasts heaving as she breathed deeply and legs twitching, and her fingers clutching desperately at nothing - at thin air.

Richardson lifted her head off his shoulder and held her upright as he undid the belt completely and pulled it away from her limp body.

'I'd give anything to have a slut like that,' Cotter breathed huskily.

'They're quite rare and very special girls,' Richardson informed him soberly, 'and they don't give themselves to just anyone.' He undid the gag and gently worked the ball out of her mouth, then wiped her wet lips with a handkerchief with paternal tenderness.

'I think Mr Cotter has become terribly aroused by you, slut,' he said. 'Perhaps you should give him a little attention; after all, he is a guest here, and I wouldn't want him to think ill of my hospitality.'

No, Gwen really didn't want to please Cotter, but she knew she really had very little choice in the matter.

'Show her how her wanton behaviour has affected you, David,' Richardson told his guest. 'She must learn to be responsible for her actions.'

Cotter needed no second invitation; he fumbled desperately with his trousers, tugged them open, and then his purple erection bobbed up in his lap as he hungrily grappled them and his underwear down to his thighs.

There was a tense pause, the only sound that of Cotter's rapid breathing, and then, knowing it was what Richardson demanded, she slipped feline-like from his lap onto the floor, and glided slowly forward on her knees.

Cotter's bulging eyes were glued to her, his mouth was hanging loosely open making him look like an imbecile, and it occurred to Gwen that despite being the prisoner it was she who was utterly in control of the man. She had, without even touching him, reduced him to a state of sweating, panting, drooling depravity. She felt a surge of contempt for him and pride in herself, then moved closer and laid her hands on his thighs. His erection jerked and he again gasped, 'Hell!'

Gwen held his trousers and pants, tugging gently, and he hastily raised his hips, letting her pull them off. He seemed utterly unaware of how stupid he appeared.

She had felt something similar towards men before, but not on such a scale; she felt a true sense of power as she slowly licked her way along his inner thigh, nuzzled his erection aside with her leather-clad face, and kissed one of his testicles. She pursed her lips, and then began to slowly apply suction until she drew it into her mouth. Her lips and tongue massaged it as his shaky hands seized her head, trying to force his erection into her mouth, but she resisted with ease.

'You have to let her perform as I've trained her,' Richardson said.

Sensing Cotter's compliance, Gwen drew his testicle in once more, again massaging it with her tongue, and then let it slowly fall from her mouth as she licked the underside of his erection and swallowed his other testicle.

'*Hell...*' Cotter moaned in disbelief. 'I'm going to come before she even gets to my cock...'

'Don't worry,' Richardson said smoothly. 'Just let her do what she does best.'

Gwen licked at his testicles further as he reached down and roughly squeezed her breasts, wincing slightly at his crudeness and force, then finally licked her way up the length of his erection and kissed the head. She pursed her lips in a gentle kiss, and then sank her mouth down over the head, letting it slide between her moist lips into the warm confines of her maw.

He came at once, groaning and bucking his hips as her tongue writhed against the underside of the head, and he went limp very shortly after that.

Gwen drew his flaccid cock into her mouth down to the base and sucked powerfully. It took little time for it to stiffen once more, and soon he was panting like a dog and begging for more. By then she was hot enough to want more herself, and as if he sensed it Richardson called her off, ordered her to turn, then lay her cheek down on the rug.

She did so, raising her buttocks and spreading her legs invitingly towards Cotter. It was an intensely degrading position so far as she was concerned - and therefore intensely arousing.

He fairly tumbled out of his chair and seized her hips, prodding his revitalised cock against her sex and thrusting desperately. Gwen tensed at the savage penetration, then gloried in it, knees spread, her pussy open and perfectly positioned.

He used her like an animal, like they were both animals, and she was soon caught up in the crude wantonness of the moment, panting for breath as her knees ground back and forth on the rug and his cock pounded furiously inside her. Through misty eyes she gazed up at Richardson, who sat passively observing.

She could feel her climax building, knew it was seconds away, and then Cotter squealed like a pig and came, slouched over her back.

Richardson motioned her to his side, so she wearily extricated herself from the sweaty tangle of Cotter's limbs and crawled forward on her belly, licking

Richardson's feet, electrified at the show she was putting on, shaking with excitement. He raised her to her feet and she spread her legs. Cotter looked on from the floor, slumped, exhausted, but still wide-eyed.

Richardson's fingers slipped inside her and his thumb stroked her clitoris. She watched Cotter, grinding her hips against Richardson's fingers, then came suddenly, arching her back, rolling her head and lewdly grinding her hips.

Shortly afterwards the gag was replaced, the dildo reinserted and the belt tightly refastened, and she was ordered to kneel at Richardson's side as the two men discussed some business and sipped brandy. Then Cotter left, with a last lecherous look at her, and she knew that he would never forget her, and that he would spend all his time searching for a girl who would behave as she did.

'Don't feel too smug,' Richardson said, slapping her on the bottom. 'He isn't much of a sophisticate, nor much of a man.'

She looked at him silently above the gag and he slowly removed it, and then led her to the bedroom. He removed the hood and belt and she sighed with relief.

'Your hair's a mess,' he said. 'Take a shower. I'll not be wanting to see you again this evening, so take an early night and get some rest.'

Gwen wanted to protest that she'd been resting all day and didn't want to go to bed, but thought better of it, and pouted sulkily as he left her alone without another word.

Chapter 8

She woke the next morning to find his hands roaming all over her body. She sighed and instinctively spread her legs as fingers gently moved down to her sex. It took almost no effort on his part to set her hips grinding and her back arching in weary pleasure, yet he held back from taking her over the edge.

Instead he clipped the leash to her collar again and led her on all fours to the kitchen. There he had her sit on her heels and clipped her wrist restraints together behind her back as he made himself breakfast. Her stomach was rumbling as she'd had no dinner the previous evening, and she licked her lips as she watched him eat. This time he gave her nothing, barely acknowledging her presence.

'Do you like it on your knees?' he asked casually.

'My knees are getting sore,' she said.

'So will your bottom if you complain,' he said tersely.

He finished his breakfast and led her into the main lounge. There he undid his trousers and made her kneel. 'I have a guest coming into town in a few days,' he said. 'I'm sure he'll enjoy the sight of such an obedient little toy presented to him.'

She raised her eyes towards him as her stomach fluttered.

'Yes,' he went on, 'I intend to let him use you as he wants.'

'I - I don't know if I can do it again,' she ventured.

'You'll do as you're told,' he said flatly. 'All the time you're here your body belongs to me. You'll do as I tell you and be enthusiastic about it.' He stood before her on the thick rug and prodded his flaccid penis against her lips. She opened her mouth instinctively, her mind still ruminating on his words.

'I think it's time we worked on your abilities in this area,' he said. 'I expect my servant to be able to fully please a man with her mouth, and a man is never fully pleased when he can't bury his entire sword in the sheath. Do you take my meaning?'

Gwen mumbled around the flesh in her mouth, not really listening to what he was saying.

'You will have to learn how to take it into your throat.' He smiled, gazing down with evident satisfaction and watching her head gliding back and forth.

'It's all mental, of course,' he went on. 'It's all about self-control, about disciplining the body.' His hips were pumping gently as he spoke, his hands firmly holding her head as he used her mouth, his glistening cock moving in and out between her tight lips.

'Just swallow as you always do.' He chuckled as he pushed deeper and she gagged weakly.

He drew back, holding her head and forcing her to bend forward and lift her chin, then thrust, his fingers tightening in her hair as he fed his erection deep into her mouth, into her throat, continuing until her nose was buried in his pubic hair, her lips were sealed around the very base of his cock, and his balls dangled against her chin.

He held himself there, holding her still as her body struggled to get accustomed to the sensations, then he slowly began to withdraw. 'Take a deep breath and get ready to swallow,' he instructed, his tone hinting at the first signs of his arousal.

Gwen moaned but he ignored her, sliding in and out of her mouth. It felt unnatural for her, but there was a certain measure of pride creeping into her thoughts, as well. He eased back and pushed forward, rhythmically, slowly pumping his cock within her throat.

'Very good,' he whispered. 'And now I want you to do all the work. I won't move.'

Gwen watched the gleaming length of his shaft as it slid slowly forward between her lips, and she accepted it, until finally inhaling deeply, closing her eyes, and easing forward all the way. She felt his cock sink into her throat, then slide deeper and deeper.

'Excellent,' he breathed. 'Very good.'

For some perverse reason Gwen was feeling a growing sense of elation at her achievement.

'I could pay a thousand dollars for a high class call-girl and still not get such expertise,' he said, the compliment thrilling her as he caressed her hair. But then he pulled out and she felt secretly disappointed - empty.

'Not so fast,' he said, his voice husky. He moved behind her, pushed down and she let her shoulders drop to the floor. Then he unclipped her wrists and guided her back up onto all fours.

'Doggy style,' he said crudely, making her feel cheap, rubbing his cock into her furrow. 'Spread your legs wider, slut, and raise your ass for me.'

She obeyed, panting with excitement, and he mounted her, shifting his grip to her hips. He ground against her raised buttocks. She sighed helplessly, wantonly, her body tingling with pleasure as his groin slapped against her bottom and his glistening shaft stabbed deep into her belly with every lunge. Her knees shuffled wider and she raised her buttocks further, swooning with pleasure as he rode her.

And he rode her savagely, tugging her hair, mauling her breasts, slapping her bottom and flanks. The climax tore at her mind and body and she let out a whimpering song of ecstasy as the pleasure swept her up and carried her to the heights of pleasure. The powerful stroke of his cock was a continuous hammer of pleasure, setting her body to shaking and trembling as he used her.

He leaned across her back, growling in her ear, hips pounding relentlessly, his erection pumping furiously inside her. She came again, her head lolling weakly, her body instinctively thrusting back against him as the pleasure screamed like a storm around her.

This time he finished even as her orgasm continued to rage, and she felt him softening with a greedy moan of despair.

'Time for you to have a little breakfast,' Richardson said, and she crawled to the kitchen after him, and ate from a bowl of milk and cereal he put on the floor.

They relaxed together in his large marble bath, Gwen wrapped in his arms as they lay back, wallowing in the fragrant warmth of the water. 'Masturbate for me,' he said languidly. His demand made her feel guilty, embarrassed, and very aroused.

'I think we should go out this evening,' he said, the water lapping gently over her hands as they moved delicately between her thighs. 'When I get back from the office.'

'Yes, sir,' she said dreamily. 'That would be nice.'

'A restaurant,' he suggested. 'Would you like to go out for dinner?'

Gwen nodded. 'I would like that very much... thank you, sir...'

The restaurant was one of those expensive haunts of the upper crust Gwen had always avoided. A string quartet played in a corner, and grey hair and conservative styles of clothing predominated.

He led her first into the bar, one of those heavy oak and leather places she tended to think of as men only clubs. There were almost no young men there at all, and few women of any age.

She sat on one of the barstools he indicated, wary of the length of the slit in her dress, while he ordered wine for them both.

'Not your kind of place, I suppose,' he said, glancing around at the various people there.

'No, not usually,' she said.

'Wait here, I'll be back,' he said without looking at her, as though he hadn't really heard her response; wasn't really interested in it.

Gwen sipped her wine, feeling a little uncomfortable by herself in the plush and hushed surroundings.

'Well, hello there,' someone crooned. A man sat next to her, taking Richardson's stool, and gazed at her with a smile of despicable self-confidence. He had a broad build just shy of fat, a rounded face and no hair. 'You working, baby?'

She stared at him in confusion, only belatedly understanding his meaning. 'No,' she snapped indignantly, 'I'm not *working*. And someone's sitting there,' she added haughtily, indicating the stool.

'Yeah, me,' he said dismissively. 'What's your name, baby?'

'Get lost,' Gwen said without looking at him, and then gratefully caught sight of Richardson returning.

'Hi,' he said to the newcomer. 'Ian Richardson.'

'George Miller. This girl yours?' the newcomer said, blunt in the extreme.

'Only when I tie her down,' Richardson said, making Gwen cringe and blush. Miller laughed.

'She's lovely on the eyes, isn't she,' Richardson went on without being prompted, putting his hands on her shoulders.

'Sure is,' Miller agreed, his eyes crawling down to her breasts. He started to vacate the stool but Richardson indicated for him to remain where he was.

'Don't get up for me,' he said amiably, 'we're not staying long. I hope Gwendolyn was polite to you while I was gone. She has a tendency to forget her manners around her betters.'

Miller looked a little confused.

'I've done my best to discipline her, you see.'

'Interesting...' Miller said slowly. 'Do any good?'

'Oh, I think so. She does mostly what she's told now, don't you, my little slut?' He dropped a hand to her hip and caressed it possessively.

'I suppose so,' she said quietly.

'That's not the answer you're supposed to give, now is it?' Richardson scolded lightly. Miller's eyes were widening as he watched Richardson's hand slip lower and rest between her thighs, pressing her dress into the tight valley between them, and then he pinched her and she started with a cute little squeal of dismay.

'Yes sir,' she whispered hastily, 'I do as I'm told, sir.'

Richardson lifted his hand and lightly touched his fingers to Gwen's lips. Then he tapped and she peeled them apart, allowing him entrance into her warm mouth. She trembled, sucking obediently, her face colouring scarlet as she saw a man on a nearby table stare, then nudge his companion who stared too, his drink hovering before his open mouth.

Richardson slipped his fingers back out. 'Don't be rude now, little slut,' he whispered. 'Take Mr Miller's hand and put it on your thigh, then let him feel up under your dress.' Her stomach lurched and she froze at the horror of being told to do such a thing in such a public place. 'Now,' Richardson growled quietly.

Miller, still staring, was clearly shocked as she reached out for his hand, but offered no resistance as she pulled it to her thigh. The ice chinked in the glass of scotch he held, but his hand moved of its own accord, sliding beneath her dress, burrowing with little finesse between her thighs and actually touching her bare pussy. The ice in his golden drink chinked even more loudly as he took a shaky sip.

'See what a slut she is, George?' Richardson mused.

Miller nodded, his voice deserting him.

'Women like this are never satisfied,' Richardson said. 'They're walking sex machines.'

Gwen still had her hand on Miller's wrist through the dress, and clutched it tightly as his fingers began to probe her sex. She slid a little further to the edge of the stool, spreading her legs, and stifled a groan as a fat finger pushed inside her.

'They have no sense of propriety,' Richardson went on casually. 'That's why they need to be disciplined, often.'

'H-how do you discipline her?' Miller asked, his voice returning as he stared transfixed at the shape of his hand beneath her dress, moving slightly between her warm thighs.

Gwen could hardly keep her hips still. Her eyes flitted from Miller's expression of deep concentration to the two men staring from the table. She wondered if anyone else had noticed the shameful behaviour at the bar, and felt a small wave of panic break against the wall of heat gripping her body.

Richardson had an arm draped casually over her shoulder, and his hand slipped down the front of her dress, casually cupping her breast as he talked. But Gwen hardly heard what Richardson was saying as he eased her off the stool and led her, an arm around her waist, out of the bar and into the main restaurant to an intimate table in one secluded corner.

A waiter arrived and Richardson ordered for them both without referring to the proffered menus, and the waiter nodded and quickly left.

'Think of poor old Miller with an erection and nowhere to put it,' he eventually said.

'Fuck Miller,' Gwen whispered vehemently.

'*Mr* Miller, to you,' he admonished smoothly. 'And I'm sure he'd approve if you did, but that won't be necessary. I think a blowjob would be sufficient.'

She pulled a face of distaste and glanced around the room, hoping Richardson would change the subject.

'I meant that,' he said.

She looked back at. 'Meant what?'

'Miller needs a blowjob. You've gotten him all excited, so it's your duty to take care of him.'

'You're the one who got him excited,' she said carefully.

'It wasn't my pussy that had him ready to pop his cork, my dear little slut,' he said with infuriating confidence.

Gwen did not like the way the conversation was going, knowing that what Richardson wanted, Richardson generally got.

'There's an alley outside,' he went on. 'Miller will be waiting for you there.'

'How... how does he—?'

'Don't ask how. Just go out to him.'

Gwen stared at him, but with little surprise. 'I - I can't...' she whispered, knowing any objection was futile.

'Of course you can. And you will. Now. Just go outside to the alley, kneel down, and give Miller what he wants.' He chuckled. 'And you can practice your deep throat if you want to see his eyes pop completely out of his head.' He sat back in his chair and smiled lazily at her. 'Go on, there's a good girl.'

'Please don't make me—'

'Now,' he said firmly. 'And then you'll be back just in time for your starters.'

Gwen rose slowly, head spinning. It was cold outside and she moved quickly into the darkened alley, wanting to get the ordeal over with quickly so she could return to the warmth and anonymity of the secluded corner in the restaurant.

She walked past a pile of green plastic garbage bags, hoping Miller had misunderstood Richardson's message - however it was transmitted. But then his darkened form stepped out from behind a large bin and he loomed over her.

'Hi baby,' he whispered hoarsely, unzipping his trousers. She dropped to her knees, shivering in the cold. His cock bobbed free, hard and thick. She engulfed it quickly and was taken completely by surprise when, with a grunt and a stab of his hips, he erupted instantly, filling her mouth with his salty emission. Such was the surprise Gwen nearly choked, but she managed to swallow and suppress the desire to gag, breathing steadily through her nose.

Miller flopped back against the damp wall, his penis hanging absurdly from his open trousers, and Gwen quickly got to her feet and scurried back into the restaurant where she found Richardson waiting at their table. Moments later the starters arrived and she ate hungrily, barely tasting the delicious food, so preoccupied was she with what had just happened. Richardson didn't speak, he merely watched her closely as he ate too.

When they had both finished Richardson silently motioned for her to rise, and then led her through to the men's room. It was empty save for one stall, and he silenced any potential questions by touching a finger to her lips, then pulled her into the second stall and locked the door.

He sat back on the toilet and pulled her forward until she was straddling him, then guided her down onto his lap. With great expertise he moved the skirt of her dress out of the way and opened his trousers. Then he folded down her bodice to bare her luscious breasts.

'Now fuck me,' he ordered, in a whisper even she could barely hear.

There was a flush from the adjacent stall and she took the opportunity to hide beneath the cover of the noise by rising slightly and then sinking down onto his standing erection. She moaned quite loudly, but managed to stifle her exclamation as the sound of churning water died on the opposite side of the flimsy partition.

Water was running into a basin a few feet away as the other man left his cubicle and washed his hands, and then the main door opened and two more men came in, chatting cheerfully.

Richardson began to suck her breasts and his hands cupped her buttocks as she rose and fell steadily on his lap. Men were talking, using the facilities, washing their hands, and yet none were aware of what was going on so close by.

Gwen's movements became more and more erratic as the heat of pleasure spread through her body. She was so aware of the men nearby but her sexual need drove all such concerns away, and in fact their close proximity only served to heighten her excitement. The need to climax was too primal, too urgent, and she trembled with lust as he chewed at her breasts.

She buried her face in the nape of his neck as she came, whimpering weakly as her pleasure rippled through her. He continued moving her limp body up and down on his turgid erection, not stopping until his own climax sent his seed flooding up into her womb, and then he began to soften.

Gwen's legs were shaky as he led her back into the restaurant, her face flushed, her eyes misty with delight. She sat for a while, eyes closed, relaxed, and barely noticed when the waiter brought their main course, and only slowly recovered enough to enjoy the beautiful cuisine. Richardson eyed her the whole time, but seemed disinclined towards conversation until after they had finished and the plates removed.

'Have you ever been with a woman?' he asked, somewhat out of the blue. 'Have you?'

'Um... no, sir,' she replied hesitantly.

'You certainly seemed interested in the shop girl - the blonde,' he observed.

'If anything I think she was interested in me, sir,' she said, blushing at the idea. 'But I don't think I'd like to do anything like that. I'm not a lesbian.'

Richardson nodded. 'Yes, she was,' he agreed with her first comment. 'But I would like to see you with another woman, despite what you may want or not.'

She thought of refusing adamantly, though secretly the idea was not altogether unappealing.

'Mmm, perhaps I'll arrange it,' he said pensively, with no consideration for her thoughts on the matter.

Chapter 9

The following morning Gwen helped Richardson shower and dress, and made him breakfast. Then he went off to various business meetings and she whiled away the long hours flopping idly about the luxury apartment.

With so much time on her hands she spent a lot of it ruminating about her situation. How on earth had she come to be there? She could still call her stepfather, promise to be a good girl and go home. The blow that would give to her pride seemed less severe than it once had. After all, her pride had taken a rather worse punishment over the course of the last few days. And what lay ahead? Richardson seemed intent on giving her to any man - or women - he chose. She was his sex toy - nothing more.

And yet, deep down, there was still something wickedly exciting about letting strangers use her, and much as she tried she could not quite suppress the quiver of excitement the thought induced.

But if she refused to be co-operative any longer Richardson would not throw her out - would he? He was enjoying himself too much - wasn't he? He didn't want to send her back to her stepfather - did he? What would he do to satisfy his strange sexual tastes then? He surely couldn't find many women like her, willing to let themselves be used and abused - could he?

And why was she letting herself be used and abused - to avoid making up with her stepfather? In less than a year she'd be able to go out on her own anyway. She could go back to him for that length of time, surely? Why was she putting up with Richardson's perversities? And worse, why was she enjoying it all so much? What was it about her that savoured such mistreatment?

No, she decided, when he returned home they were going to have a frank discussion about what she would and would not do to please him. They could play his games, but on her terms. Yes, that made sense. And he would have to do as she wished, wouldn't he? Otherwise she'd leave; she'd just walk out with her head held high.

So, having decided upon that, Gwen thought about how she could refuse him and what she would do if she left. But the thought of leaving depressed her a little. It would mean going back to her stepfather and being a good girl, but worse, she admitted, it would mean no more of Richardson's wicked games; she was not at all sure how far she wanted them to go, and wasn't fond of every aspect of what he did, but the thought of life without them was depressing in its boring sameness.

Late in the afternoon Gwen heard the faint sound of the lift rising and tried to remember the speech she'd been rehearsing, laying down a few ground rules for Richardson to adhere to. But then the brash confidence she'd been building all day suddenly deserted her; what would he do if she suddenly started making demands and telling him what he could and couldn't do?

Gwen almost shrieked with shock when the lounge door opened and a woman strutted in. Richardson came in right behind her, which eased some of the shock, but as the woman walked over to gaze disparagingly at Gwen she found herself almost shrinking back under the haughty scrutiny.

Although attractive, with short blonde hair, the woman's demeanour was one of aggression, and the suit she wore clearly covered a fit and powerful body. She considered Gwen with a look of scorn and a predatory hunger. 'So, this is your newest little toy,' she said, her voice deep and masculine.

'Lovely, isn't she?' Richardson said. The woman said nothing, neither agreeing nor disagreeing. 'I just knew you'd be perfect for breaking her in to the whims of a woman,' he went on.

The woman smirked down at Gwen. 'Just remember the rules,' she said to him over her shoulder. 'You touch me and I'll break you in half.'

Richardson nodded and smiled, holding his hands up in mock surrender.

'W-what's going on?' Gwen asked timidly.

'What's going on is that my friend here is going to teach you how to please another woman,' Richardson told her.

'No,' she gasped.

'Oh yes,' the woman said with an avaricious glint in her eye, moving to where Gwen cowered back on the sofa.

'No... no,' Gwen murmured, slowly shaking her head in denial, clutching the silk robe she wore tighter around herself.

The woman sat on the sofa beside her, grinning broadly, then reached out and gripped Gwen's wrist tightly in a powerful fist.

'Please, let me go,' the startled girl begged quietly.

'I love that cute English accent,' the woman smirked, and then stood and dragged Gwen to her feet. 'Stay still if you know what's good for you,' she warned curtly, spinning Gwen around. 'Now, you're going to be a good girl, aren't you?' she hissed in Gwen's ear. 'I'm going to tell you what to do, and you're going to do it.'

Gwen tried to think of a response.

'And you will answer me when I speak to you, and you will call me, mistress. Do you understand, little slut?'

'Y-yes,' Gwen whispered fearfully. 'I understand, mistress.'

'Good...' the woman drooled, and then before Gwen could counter the move she snatched both her wrists and pinned them together behind her back, gripping them excruciatingly in one fist while she methodically unbuttoned her double-breasted jacket. 'Now then,' she said slowly as she unbuckled the leather belt she had exposed and a long slow tug made it hiss menacingly as it passed through the loops of her trousers, 'it would seem you need to learn a few manners.'

Gwen squealed, her clamped wrists protesting and the strained tendons in her legs burning as the woman lifted her arms and bent her forward, deftly swinging the belt into a loop and gripping the folded strip of leather in one hand.

Richardson moved close and started to stroke Gwen's hair as the brute of a woman raised her arm, took deliberate aim, and then swept the cruel leather down against the poor girl's bottom, the only protection afforded it being the delicate silk of the robe she wore. Gwen caught her breath as the pain seared into her buttocks, and then despite her determination not to give the loathsome pair the satisfaction of hearing her beg, shrieked for mercy.

But the belt cut through the air and bit again, shunting Gwen forward, his hands still stroking her hair in a charade of comforting her. The woman lifted Gwen's wrists higher and the pain tore into her shoulders and biceps, but paled in comparison to the pain delivered by the belt.

And then the fingers entwined in her hair lifted her head, and she was staring through blurred eyes at Richardson's free hand undoing his expensively cut trousers, and despite her anguish, there was a dark pleasure beginning to accompany the pain.

Then a turgid erection was pulsing before her flushed face and prodding against her lips. 'Go on,' the woman urged, 'open your mouth and do what you do best, little slut.'

Gwen hesitated, but the belt swept down again and cracked into her bottom, and with a sigh her lips peeled open, Richardson moved his hips in, and her mouth filled with his rigid flesh, her lips straining wider apart as it entered.

'Good girl,' the woman whispered huskily. 'I knew you'd love it. Is it tasty? It's certainly what I consider a good use for that pretty little mouth of yours.' The woman knelt, her face close to Gwen's. 'Mmm... he's in your throat, isn't he?' she taunted, and then caressed Gwen's throat as Richardson pushed himself fully into her mouth and ground his groin against her face, hissing with pleasure as her eyelashes fluttered against his belly.

'Does it make you feel proud?' the woman went on. 'Does it taste good? Suck him. Suck him like a good little slut. Let him use your mouth like a cunt. Let him fuck you there. And maybe if you're good he'll move behind and fuck your pussy. Would you like that, sweetie? You love this, don't you? I can tell.' Then she moved her face in even closer, gently kissing Gwen's ear, nibbling her earlobe and then licking down the taut tendons of her throat. 'Mmm,' she cooed, 'I can feel him inside there, pulsing and wanting to come. You're a dirty girl doing that to him,' she whispered. 'You're a dirty little tramp. Suck his cock, baby. Swallow it all.'

Richardson was pumping steadily, and then the woman stood and the belt struck again, causing Gwen to rock forward and almost gag as the cock in her mouth stabbed to the back of her throat. The belt swept down six more times, rending muted squeals from the bent girl who was having to breathe deeply through her nose to fill her lungs, and as she did her breasts swelled into the waiting palms of Richardson, which massaged her soft flesh through the silk robe as he ground his hips languidly.

And then the beating stopped and the only sounds in the room were that of the slightly out of breath woman, and the wet rhythmic suckling as Richardson's erection pumped slowly in and out of Gwen's mouth. Then the belt dropped to the floor and a strong hand caressed Gwen's sore bottom through the silk, causing her to moan around the stalk stretching her lips. The woman still held her wrists firmly and high, and now the belt was no longer inflicting its bite the pain burned into Gwen's shoulders and arms once again. Her other hand moved roughly over Gwen's behind, massaging and kneading her buttocks. And then a finger insinuated itself into the deep valley between her buttocks, and pressed rudely against her rear entrance.

'Mmm, what a lovely tight hole, sweetie,' the woman purred. 'Such promise. Do you like being used there? Oh, I bet you do. I bet you'd love your master to screw you there right now. Wouldn't you? Sure you would. Dirty girls love being screwed there. I bet you're aching for it, aren't you, baby?'

Then an insistent thumb replaced the finger, and the finger worked its way further down. It stroked through the silk, entering slightly between Gwen's sex lips, which were treacherously wet, taking the material with it. As the thumb probed the finger found her clitoris and Gwen squealed with a cocktail of pleasure and shame around the column of flesh nudging into her throat. Richardson exhaled slowly, moving his hips back until just the head of his cock was lodged between her lips, and then sinking forward again in unison with the long slow hiss that escaped his lungs. Gwen could hear the wet silk being worked between her thighs, deeper and deeper into her sex.

'Hear that, slut?' the woman goaded, as though understanding what Gwen was feeling and hearing. 'That's your pussy. It's all wet now.'

It mortified Gwen to know the woman was manipulating her with such ease. She could feel the heaviness in her loins, the throbbing in her groin. She knew she was wet, that the woman's treatment of her was turning her body traitor to her attempted resistance.

Then the fingers left her and she heard a shuffling, and knew exactly what was coming. The silk was folded up onto her hips and she felt the woman kneeling behind her, the material of her jacket rubbing the backs of her legs. The woman still gripped Gwen's wrists with one hand, but peeled her sex open with the other as though savouring the prospect of a tasty morsel to devour, and then the bent girl squealed as a long squirming muscle burrowed inside her. Gwen was being licked and sucked by another woman!

She tried vainly to protest, but the cock in her mouth reduced her curses upon the woman to nothing more than a mumbled wail, and the standing man and kneeling woman took their enjoyment at their leisure. The woman lapped expertly, finding Gwen's clitoris and coaxing the poor girl towards a wonderful orgasm with contemptuous ease. Gwen despised the woman, but her resolution to resist her crumbled quickly and shamefully. From her enforced crouch she ached abominably, and yet her hips instinctively edged back and her scorched buttocks moulded against the woman's face, silently urging the tongue to greater efforts. Despite the pain and the degradation the pair were deliberately heaping upon her - or perhaps because of it - her insides were knotting with an exquisite masochistic pleasure. It was as if the more demeaning her behaviour the more wicked and shocking, and thus arousing, it was.

'You pay attention to what I'm doing, slut,' the woman panted, briefly breaking away from the juicy morsel. 'You'll be doing the same soon... to me.' And then the insistent tongue invaded her again, probing incredibly deep within her. It caressed the sides of her vaginal sleeve with shocking intimacy, pumping in and out in a way that had the bewildered girl swooning and incoherently begging for more. Then it pulled back and began to work over her clitoris again, and Gwen shuddered to an exhausting orgasm, sucking avidly on the flesh in her mouth and squirming back onto the woman's hot face.

'Whore,' the lesbian sneered, pulling back from the lewd embrace, her lips and chin glistening with the girl's succulent juices.

Gwen was in a daze and only vaguely aware as the two disengaged and changed places, the grip on her wrists never abating. Then strong fingers were in her hair again and lifting her head, and she saw the woman no longer wore her trousers, and she was naked beneath.

'I-I hate you,' she panted.

'Yes, right, of course you do,' the woman said patiently. 'Now in a moment you will do for me what I just did for you... you will lick me.' She cupped Gwen's chin, holding her head up as she stared down unblinkingly into her glistening eyes. Gwen felt Richardson's cock pushing against her nether hole, and then her frozen expression crumpled and the woman grinned triumphantly as he sank into Gwen's bottom with one long smooth penetration, shunting her ever closer to the woman's wet and swollen sex lips.

'Yessss,' the woman hissed. 'It's so sweet, isn't it? You love it, don't you, honey? You live for it. Say it, naughty girl, say it. Tell me how you love it.'

'I...' Gwen gurgled, 'I...'

'Say it,' the gloating woman insisted. 'Tell me.'

Gwen opened her mouth to speak, but then winced as Richardson thrust deep and hard, impaling her on his thick erection.

'I - I love it!' she gasped.

'And where do you love it, my little English flower? Where?'

'In my... in my...'

'In your ass,' the woman prompted. 'Say it. You love being fucked in your ass.'

'Yesss...' Gwen gasped raggedly. 'I love being fucked in my ass!'

The woman smiled victoriously down upon her victim, watching her; eyes closed, cheeks flushed, forehead damp with perspiration as she rocked back and forth under the steady movements of Richardson's hips. And then she pressed her groin against that beautiful flushed face, swamping her in humid, pungent shadow. 'Pretty girl,' she whispered, stroking the hair away from Gwen's damp forehead and caressing her cheek with paradoxical tenderness. 'Suck me, pretty girl. Eat my cunt.'

With her world in a complete daze Gwen kissed and licked, not really knowing how to please the woman, but letting instinct lead her.

'Deeper,' the woman encouraged. 'Mmm, that's very good...'

Gwen licked her clitoris experimentally, strumming it with the tip of her tongue, and despite her abhorrence she was gratified to induce a shudder and a sigh from the masculine female. Soon she was licking to the woman's obvious and immense satisfaction, for she began to grind her hips with less and less control, sighing with pleasure as Gwen's tongue lapped steadily at her soaking and pungent sex, working steadily, wanting to prove to the woman that she could give her pleasure.

Gwen whimpered and moaned with each shunt from Richardson, her rectum full with his erection. The sensations permeating her body seemed to alter, narrowing their focus and seeping deeper into her flesh, deeper into her soul. She found herself shuffling her legs wider, even though doing so put more pressure on her aching shoulders and straining arms.

She knew she was going to climax again - to climax from the avaricious cock possessing her bottom and the taste and feel of the demanding woman. And she was consumed with pleasing and being pleased, with the heat and hunger in her sex and the taste of the other woman's pussy on her tongue.

There was no room for complicated thoughts; she was a creature of instinct, of raw lust and desire. She whimpered into the flesh smothering her face, gasping and panting and sobbing as she lapped desperately at the woman's slick sex.

And the woman came, groaning with a low, gravely sound, clutching at Gwen's head, urging her sex against her tongue and lips as she bucked furiously. Gwen continued to lick and suck, knowing she must - and wanting to.

Eventually the woman stepped to the side, still pinning Gwen's wrists above her back, and Gwen's head lolled down. She moaned as Richardson's movements became more frantic and less controlled, and then heard him gurgle as he erupted deep inside her, his groin glued to her smarting buttocks as he ejaculated forcefully, and the woman chuckled.

Chapter 10

'Now what should I do with you?' the woman mused, gazing down at her delicious captive with a sinister smile flitting across her lips.

She scanned the little dungeon room, and then moved across to the shelves, picking up and examining some whips, crops, switches and paddles. Then she picked up a ball-gag and examined it, then moved back to Gwen. With a surprisingly swift move she gripped Gwen's hair and pulled her up to her feet, then as Gwen's mouth opened to protest she wedged the ball inside. Gwen gurgled and gasped as the woman's strong fingers worked the whole of the ball in, stretching her jaw and pressing her tongue down uncomfortably.

The woman smirked, then pulled the leather strap around behind Gwen's head and buckled it tightly in place. 'This will rest your tongue for the more important tasks ahead,' she chuckled, then turned back to the shelf and plucked a small chain from it, and Gwen looked down anxiously as the woman held one end against her right nipple, instantly recognising the purpose of the small clamp and trying to brace herself for the sharp pain that would inevitably follow.

Her plaintive whimper into the gag was muffled, and she grimaced around the ball that held her mouth open as the clamp bit cruelly into her erect bud. The other end of the chain was then raised and the second clamp bit into her other poor nipple.

The woman leered with satisfaction, and then curled a finger with malicious intent around the middle of the chain's span between the two youthful breasts and slowly lifted it up and out.

Gwen cried out again as the clamps pulled excruciatingly on her nipples and bit even deeper. She was forced forward, and then up onto her toes as the woman gleefully lifted the chain higher, and as she continued the anguish for Gwen mounted, her nipples throbbing and drawing tears to her eyes.

'You're lovely, aren't you?' the woman cooed, watching Gwen squirm and try vainly to alleviate the pain. 'You're so lovely... and so soft.'

With her free hand she cupped the underside of Gwen's breasts and stroked them alternately, her gaze upon them, a distant look in her eyes, and for a terrible moment Gwen wondered at her sanity. Then the woman moved backwards and Gwen squealed as she was forced to shuffle forward after her to desperately try to ease the pull on her savagely pinched nipples. A moment later the woman pinned Gwen back against a wall and forced a leg between her thighs, and then strong fingers took possession of her pussy, spreading her lips. She produced another small clamp, eagerly showing Gwen the small alligator jaws attached by a short chain to a small metal weight, then her malicious grin broadened as she moved it down with intense deliberation.

At first Gwen did not understand, for she already had clamps on both nipples, then as the glinting object moved down and between her thighs her eyes widened and she cried around the gag in denial. She tried frantically to twist aside but the woman held her easily, her fingers rubbing at her treacherously swollen clitoris. Gwen felt the cold bite of the metal clamp squeezing against her and whimpered helplessly, begging the woman with her eyes. But she only grinned back, adjusted it carefully, then let the jaws snap shut.

Gwen almost crumpled to the floor and thought she would faint, but the woman's bulk pinned her to the uncompromising wall, a dizzying wave of nausea churning in her belly. The woman moved back and Gwen did indeed drop weakly to her knees, tears filling her eyes and meandering down her cheeks, gasping and sobbing with outrage as the pain consumed her.

'Weak,' the woman sneered contemptuously. 'You're lovely, but weak. I despise weakness in people.' She gripped and lifted the chain again and Gwen simpered once more, forced to her feet by the pull on her nipples. Then a long chain was attached to the centre of the one spanning Gwen's breasts and she had little choice but to follow, every movement setting the weight between her thighs swinging and pulling at her clitoris.

Gwen sobbed hopelessly as she staggered after the woman to the entrance hall.

'Ah, I thought I saw these on my way in,' the woman said, picking up a pair of stiletto heels. 'Just what I want to show off your lovely legs and pretty little ass.'

Following the unspoken order, Gwen stepped into them gingerly and then stood obediently while the woman moved around her, examining the mouth-watering effect the heels had on her shapely form.

'Very, very nice,' she said, giving Gwen's buttocks a squeeze. 'Marvellous.'

She summoned the lift and then led her charge inside. Gwen looked out desperately, searching vainly for signs of Richardson, but he was nowhere to be seen as the doors silently slid shut.

'Looking for your master?' the woman goaded. 'Forget it. He often loans out his girls to us, and we return the favour; now and then we give him one of our naughty little lesbians to use.' She sniggered unkindly. 'Some of them really hate having to submit to a man, so it keeps them in their place. He does a good job.'

The lift doors opened, but not onto the private garage. Instead they revealed the lobby of the building, glinting expensively with many mirrors, and marble, and chandeliers overhead.

The lobby was long and narrow with large glass doors etched with gold at the end, and for the second time in her life Gwen found herself completely naked on a city street. Thankfully, this one was a quiet side street with no traffic passing by. Nevertheless, Gwen felt in a state of shock as the woman led her across the pavement to a waiting car. She was bundled into the back seat, then the woman climbed in beside her and the car pulled away from the kerb.

As with Richardson's limousine the windows were tinted, but a woman drove. She was a thin-faced brunette, and she regarded Gwen scornful in the rear-view mirror before shaking her head and returning her eyes to the road ahead.

The journey passed in silence, Gwen trying to understand what was happening to her, where she was going or why she was permitting it. Not that she had any say, of course.

The car eventually turned onto a narrow tree-lined street and came to a stop before the canopied entrance of a place called *Sappho's*. She had no idea what the place was about, for the small plaque and blank door gave no indication. But while she was gazing uncertainly at the building the woman opened the rear door of the car and climbed out, then tugged on the chain to force Gwen to scramble after her. Thankfully the pavement was deserted.

Fluorescent lights brightly lighted the interior of the club. The entrance corridor was narrow and utilitarian stone, but there were several people moving around, and all turned to regard Gwen as she was led amongst them. Gwen's face flamed.

'Hello ladies, see the little fish I caught?' the woman said jovially.

One, an older woman, shook her head in apparent disgust and walked on, but several others wandered closer to examine Gwen.

'Where'd you get her, Carol?' one asked.

'She belongs to Richardson,' the woman - Carol - informed the questioner. 'He loaned her to us. Said she needs a little exposure; she's too shy.'

Several of the women sniggered at that, and one reached out to give Gwen's breasts a cold squeeze.

'Poor baby,' another said in mock sympathy.

Gwen yelped indignantly as someone pinched her bottom, twisting around to see who had taken the liberty, but that set the weight swaying on her clitoris and she yelped again. Then someone nudged the weight to set it swinging harder and the group of women laughed as her discomfort mounted.

'Pathetic creature,' one said scornfully.

'Going to hand her around, Carol?' asked another.

'Only to people who ask very nicely,' Carol replied, but it was all just too much for Gwen. She couldn't take it any more. One shock to her system had followed another and she swayed dazedly, but then the chain tugged sharply on her nipples and Carol was pulling her further along the corridor. The woman let the chain dangle over her right shoulder, smirking and greeting other women they met along the way as Gwen hurried along behind her, whimpering into the gag and quaking under the eyes of every woman they passed.

Carol turned and led her through a door into a locker room, then over to where hooks lined the wall. She threw the chain over one hook, and then tugged it so Gwen was forced up onto her toes before tying it off.

'You wait there, sweetie,' she said, giving Gwen's bottom an intimate squeeze.

She moved only a few feet away to a row of lockers, and there opened one and began to strip. Once naked she returned to take Gwen's chain, and then led her through another door and along a narrower and lower corridor, the atmosphere heavy with the smell of chlorinated water and the air warm and clinging.

Carol picked up a large towel and wrapped it around herself, tying it over her breasts and beneath her armpits, then continued on and pushed into another room. Rolling heat struck Gwen like a wall and she gasped for breath as it pervaded her lungs.

They were in a small sauna. It was circular in shape, with two levels of wooden benches lining the wall. In the centre was a round vent that dropped from the low ceiling, with steam billowing lazily from it and drifting around the room.

There were already several women there, naked, sitting on their towels. Two were older looking, but the third seemed to be about Gwen's age and had a pretty elfin face, a dainty body, and lovely long blonde hair.

'Look what followed you in, Carol,' one of the older women said, her voice sounding strangely mute in the dull atmosphere.

'She's on loan to me,' Carol gloated. 'I'm to teach her not to be so shy, so I thought I'd show her off to you all.'

The three women looked more than a little interested to hear this, and their body-language made it clear to Gwen that each of them would like to get their hands - and much else besides - on her.

Carol dropped her towel and joined her friends on one of the benches, leaving Gwen standing directly on her own, feeling terribly exposed, although the subdued lighting helped retain just a little of her modesty. The steam drifted around her, and within seconds her hair was wet and plastered to her forehead and her body glistened enticingly with perspiration.

'Cute,' one of the women said.

The door opened quietly and two more entered, one a tall black woman with a shaven head, the other a chunky Hispanic. They joined the others, draping themselves on the wooden slatted benches, loosening their towels and eyeing Gwen appreciatively.

Carol began to relate what had happened in Richardson's apartment, taking great and particular pains to describe how she had taught Gwen to lick her pussy so successfully.

Oddly, Gwen was no longer feeling quite so mortified under the lecherous scrutiny as she had only a few minutes before. Perhaps that was because the other women were also naked, or perhaps she was simply growing accustomed to being in such humiliating predicaments.

As the heat in the small chamber increased the metal adornments clinging to Gwen's nipples and clitoris burned her tender flesh, making her move slightly to alleviate the ever-present discomfort. She was coated with beads of perspiration now, dribbling into her eyes and making her blink. She was having difficulty breathing and her shoulders sagged weakly as the gathered women seemed to lose a little interest in her and started chatting in hushed tones in the oppressive little room.

Left alone and no longer the centre of attention, Gwen started to ponder the events of recent days. She had begun to realise there was a masochistic side to her nature, a masochistic side Richardson was unearthing and bringing into the light. That side to her nature revelled in the abuse she had been subjected to, in playing the part of the tormented innocent. The shocking lewdness of Richardson's mistreatment seemed to stoke her inner fires more than anything she had ever experienced in her life.

He simultaneously made her into an object of total sexual desire and robbed her of any guilt for whatever was done with that desire. For as a victim she could not, of course, bear any responsibility. Without guilt her inhibitions faded, and she was free to be the true sensual hedonist she wanted to be, with any man - or woman - who wanted her.

Her inhibitions did only fade, though. They remained simmering just beneath the surface as the women's attention reverted to her and the muted talking stopped, yet they inspired more depraved excitement than dread. Her eyes flitted from one hungry face to another, all staring at her, all lusting after her. They all wanted to use her for their own questionable pleasure, of that there was no mistake. She could neither hide nor protect herself from their cruel attentions, and a part of her basked in that knowledge.

'Brianna,' Carol said quietly to the pretty blonde who was one of the three originally present, 'I want to see you with my Gwendolyn. Make her come.'

'Me?' Brianna looked surprised, but not displeased with the request of the older woman. Despite finding her very attractive, Gwen eyed her warily whilst trying to blink the perspiration out of her eyes.

There was a heavy pause as everyone in the hot chamber waited, and then the blonde slipped with an ease of movement off the bench and glided gracefully through the steamy atmosphere to Gwen. 'Poor girl,' she cooed, gazing down at the nipple clamps that pinched so tightly. Slowly reaching up she unclipped them and let the chain fall, and Gwen groaned into the gag with relief as the blood returned and her nipples pulsed agonisingly.

The girl smiled and slid her hands up over Gwen's shoulders, then behind her head. She pressed her own shapely body against Gwen, and Gwen swooned with delight as another female's naked breasts moulded softly to her own, calming and soothing the awful throbbing. The sympathetic embrace was so comforting she thought she might cry, but then the girl gently kissed her throat and up to her ear and a frisson of sexual excitement overwhelmed that self-indulgent response, and she relaxed in the girl's arms as her warm lips meandered down until they could cocoon one of Gwen's punished nipples.

The girl sucked very tenderly, her tongue feather-soft as it coasted across and around each sensitive pink nub. Her hands stroked Gwen's back, then moved down to her bottom, cupping and caressing both buttocks.

Unfair comments of derision came from the watchers, making Gwen cringe anew with shame, but there was nothing she could do to stop the girl who mouthed her nipples so beautifully. Both pert buds were oversensitive due to the effect of the clamps, and the protesting nerves responded enthusiastically to such gentle treatment. Soft, throbbing heat sank deep into her breasts and then began to sink even deeper into the core of her body.

The girl moved downward, licking a taunting path down Gwen's fluttering belly until she knelt before her. She reached for the final clamp and slipped it off, and Gwen's back arched as fresh pain emanated from her sex. The girl did not touch her clitoris, gently massaging her thighs instead while waiting for the pain to ease.

Then she slowly moved inwards, running her tongue up and down against the edges of Gwen's sex lips, then slowly peeling them open like a juicy fruit and slipping her tongue inside.

Gwen moaned and tried with little conviction to twist away, unable to escape the smirking faces and staring eyes surrounding her. She shook her head, horrified and yet enthralled by such intimate violation in front of an audience of strangers, but with such wonderful things happening between her thighs there was nothing she could do to resist.

The sneering eyes seemed to drown her, whispered voices taunting and sniggering, the occasional finger pointing accusingly.

She cried out, her hips jerking back as the girl's tongue flicked across her swollen clitoris, and a satisfied chorus of hushed laughter and taunts instantly accompanied her wanton reaction.

The girl, Brianna, raised her hands slowly up the back of Gwen's trembling thighs, pressing her splayed fingers into Gwen's tensed buttocks, squeezing eagerly as her expert tongue began to ravish her clitoris, and Gwen groaned helplessly into the gag, feeling as though her insides were being consumed.

One of the girl's fingers probed tentatively at the tiny portal to Gwen's bottom, a neat nail scratching delicately, and then pressed up into her rectum. Another followed, accompanying the first, and then a third pressed in. She pumped gently in and out as she licked and sucked, and a new wave of humiliation swept across Gwen's shattered consciousness as she realised the girl was deliberately being extreme for the benefit of the watching women. She trembled and sighed, her mind in a dazed sexual stupor.

The girl's mouth engulfed her sex, her lips kissing, her tongue stroking, her teeth nibbling, and all those women watched, the mocking comments doing little to disguise the raw hunger in their eyes and hushed tones.

Gwen's groin moved instinctively against the lovely kneeling girl's face, her head lolled back and her unfocused, unseeing eyes stared up at the low ceiling, the steam drifting around her, the perspiration glistening in the subdued lighting as it dripped down her glowing body. She sagged weakly, her thighs resting against the shoulders and breasts of Brianna, only her hips moving, slowly gyrating, and her sex a pit of need and heat as the girl continued to apply her mouth with dangerous proficiency.

Gwen was going to come. Confused thoughts spun in her head at the knowledge, but there was simply little care left in her. All but pleasure had been crowded out by the desperate yearning for sexual satiation.

One of the women stood and quietly moved behind her. Gwen hardly noticed, even when the woman worked the gag out of her mouth. Now she could protest. Now she could demand they release her, demand they stop molesting her... but she simply sighed wearily with intense pleasure.

'Sing, pretty girl, sing,' someone coaxed.

The orgasm swept over her, rolling and roaring like a tidal wave engulfing the shore. It was relentless and she knew it couldn't be suppressed; felt the sheer power of it as it swept in.

She screamed. Even as she did so she knew an embarrassment, and yet she could not help herself, could not stop the raw scream of ecstasy as her innards erupted with bliss. Her plaintive wail rose in a languid climb up the scale of wonder, easing back only to redouble in strength. She spent her last breath on a whimper of pleasure, and then inhaled a deep ragged breath and cried out once more.

All those eyes; watching, missing nothing. All those ears; listening, equally alert to Gwen's wanton display.

They murmured their approval and Gwen sagged against the kneeling girl, exhausted, her eyes closed. She felt hands on her but hardly took notice, sagging to the floor as the girl slipped silently away, and despite wanting nothing more than to curl up in a quiet corner and lose herself in sleep, she found herself positioned on her knees in front of Carol, the woman's legs spread wide as she was guided in between them by unseen hands.

Without being told, but knowing what was expected of her, she began to lick, weakly at first. Then as her mind began to reassemble its scattered pieces she tried to twist back, but the onlookers would have none of it and a sharp slap on the bottom nudged her mouth back to the woman's waiting sex. She felt hands crawling all over her, mauling between her legs, molesting her breasts, kneading her buttocks and probing inquisitively at her tiny rear opening.

Yet she could do nothing but lick and suck at the woman's sopping sex, for the hands that possessed her were too demanding and she had little spirit left with which to defy them. But even though exhausted and suffering the unwelcome attention of the women, Gwen felt a seed of satisfaction germinating in the depths of her soul as Carol began to grind her buttocks down against the floor and groan with delight. But then she was pulled roughly aside, barely getting a glimpse at the face of the new woman before she was forced between her thighs, there to lick once again. Fingers, sometimes one or two, sometimes more, from different hands with different demands, penetrated her.

The second woman came quickly, shuddering and desperately clawing Gwen's hair, and then she was moved to the next. She too seized Gwen's hair, tugging and manoeuvring her head with unnecessary aggression as she ordered the bewildered girl to please her. Gwen protested but obeyed, the sexual heat gripping her strongly, increasing with her feeling of being used.

Then strong hands seized the dazed, exhausted girl and flung her onto her back on the warm floor. Another woman covered her, entwining their legs and avidly grinding her sex back and forth against Gwen's, who groaned with both pleasure and discomfort as her body was manipulated into positions to please the avaricious woman and her cohorts, smothering the exhausted, sweating, supine girl as they continued to use her limp body in the sweltering room.

Eventually they were all sated and it was over. Gwen was led, crawling, out of the sauna to a shower room, where she knelt on all fours as Carol washed her with refreshing soap and rinsed her off. She was dried in a fluffy towel and given water to drink, and then the gag was fed back into her mouth. The clips were placed on her aching nipples again and Carol, now dressed in her suit, led her to an airy entrance hall, the main glass doors on the left and a reception desk on the right. A young and stylishly dressed female sat behind the desk, raising her eyes as Carol and her weary charge appeared.

'This is the main entrance, Carol,' she said, frowning.

'I know that very well,' Carol replied, glaring at the younger female, 'and we'll only be a minute.' She looked out of a window as Gwen stood quietly and obediently, too exhausted to be embarrassed at the disapproval the receptionist was directing her way. Then a door behind the reception desk opened and an older woman appeared. She looked to be in her forties, elegant and stunning, with beautifully styled short dark hair. She wore a dark and expensive business suit with a knee-length skirt, and bore an impatient and regal air as she strode towards them.

She examined Gwen quickly but thoroughly, then gave Carol a nod. 'All right, April is bringing the car round to the front. Put her in the trunk and do it quickly.'

Carol bobbed her head respectfully but the woman had already turned her eyes back to Gwen. She reached out and gripped her chin between a delicate but firm thumb and forefinger, raising it and frowning, her gaze never wavering. 'She looks tired,' she commented. 'Have you been using her too roughly?' she asked Carol, her eyes never leaving Gwen's face.

'Sure,' Carol said with evident satisfaction.

'She'll do anyway,' the cultured woman confirmed. 'Take her.'

Carol led Gwen to the door and then outside as a luxury blue car smoothed up to the pavement and a female driver with lovely red hair got out. There were some people about, but not near enough to notice or concern Gwen.

'Ms Brook wants her in the trunk,' Carol informed the driver, who opened the boot of the car as Carol tugged on the leash. Alarm suddenly gripped Gwen when she realised their intention, but she was too slow and too tired to resist as the two women manhandled her into the unwelcoming space and slammed the boot shut.

She found herself in claustrophobic darkness. A few seconds later the car moved forward, and she wonder with mounting trepidation where she was going and who the austere woman who had clearly instigated this whole abduction was. But eventually exhaustion caught up with her and she dozed a little, despite her discomfort in the dark cramped confines of the boot, and the worry of where she was being taken.

'Hello, had a nice ride?' the driver said. 'Let's get you out of there,' she went on without awaiting a response, reaching for Gwen, who sat awkwardly, feeling stiff and sore, and with the driver's help managed to climb out of the boot.

They were in a double garage, the doors closed, there was no sign of the odious Carol, and she had absolutely no idea where they were.

'Come on then,' the driver said, taking her chain and tugging it experimentally. She giggled as they pulled on Gwen's nipples, and then moved around the front of the car towards a single door. Gwen, of course, had no choice but to follow, and they emerged into a luxurious house. The driver led her to a sweeping staircase and they ascended, and then walked along the landing to a bedroom.

It was a large room, with a four-poster bed complete with canopy, several large chests and wardrobes, a group of chairs gathered around a fireplace, and a large walnut desk set before the drawn curtains.

The driver drew back the covers of the bed and made Gwen lie down. Then she unclipped the leash and removed the cruel nipple and clitoris clamps, much to Gwen's relief. She then gently worked the gag out of Gwen's aching mouth.

'Want a drink?' she asked.

Gwen worked her jaw slowly, wincing a little, but nodded gratefully. The driver went into an adjoining bathroom and returned with a refreshing glass for her.

Once Gwen had eagerly drained it the driver pulled the covers over her. 'Have a little bit of a rest,' she said kindly, puffing up the pillow beneath Gwen's head.

'Where am I?' Gwen ventured to ask, but the driver merely moved away and left, quietly closing the door behind her, and Gwen was sure she heard a key turning in the lock.

Knowing there would be no chance of getting away, Gwen resigned herself to the fact and looked around at the comfortable surroundings, then turned off the bedside lamp and settled down, slightly anxious but telling herself she had already been through the worst.

Chapter 11

Gwen had no idea what time it was when she woke up. The redhead who had driven the car was there, and having turned on the bedside lamp she pulled back the covers.

'Come on, time to get ready,' she said.

'Ready? For what?' Gwen asked groggily.

'Art, of course,' the redhead said simply, as though Gwen should understand what she was talking about.

'Art?'

Without another word the redhead took Gwen's arm, guided her out of bed and led her back down the stairs to a large open room that had clearly been prepared for a gathering of some sort. There were a number of oddly shaped devices scattered around, along with a number of sculptures on small pedestals. The sculptures were of an erotic nature as, it seemed, were the strange devices.

One in particular caught Gwen's attention, and not only because the redhead was leading her to it. It was a tall but narrow box made of shocking pink plastic, clearly hollow, for there were several openings cut into its front and back. The back was opened and the redhead motioned Gwen closer.

'Ah, there you are, April.' The cultured lady from the club appeared as though from nowhere, now dressed in a lovely black evening gown, followed by another girl in a maid's uniform. She looked at Gwen happily, nodding her head. 'She should be just about perfect,' she mused, her eyes sparkling.

'For what?" Gwen asked.

The woman smiled, and then turned her towards the box without answering. It was a little taller than Gwen, and a little wider than her hips and shoulders. The woman pushed her in until her firm breasts went through two perfectly positioned round holes cut into the front.

There was a smaller round opening at the height of her mouth, with four plastic pins bordering it, two above and two below.

'Open your mouth, girl, and press your lips to the wall,' the woman ordered, and without waiting for Gwen to obey she nudged the back of her head. Gwen had to open her mouth to avoid the pins and they entered between her teeth, keeping her mouth open. Then a strap was passed around her head and fastened in place, keeping her mouth held wide open over the hole.

Gwen tried to twist back but her arms were quickly strapped to the sides of the box, and then her legs were pulled apart and her ankles strapped apart too. The back section was then swung closed, and she grunted as it pushed in against her, sealing her effectively inside the cramped shell. It was an extremely tight fit, and even with her breasts pushed out through the holes at the front there was barely room for her inside. And then Gwen realised that the rear section also had a hole shaped into it, and through that her bottom protruded, naked and vulnerable.

'Excellent,' she heard the woman purr with approval, and then a moment later she felt a touch on her sex, which she immediately realised was accessible through another hole cut into the front of the box, just large enough to let an inquisitive hand slip through. She then felt a finger stroke her tongue and instinctively tried to close her mouth, only to be foiled by the plastic pins. She tried to protest, but all that emerged was an incoherent warbling.

'Relax, darling,' she heard. 'It won't be forever, and not every girl gets to be a piece of art.'

Soft music began to play, and after a while Gwen heard more and more voices, the babble rising around her. Hands stroked, squeezed and massaged her buttocks fairly frequently - and sometimes slapped them as well. Other hands slipped into the small hole cut before her pussy to stroke or explore her sex, and her breasts were casually caressed and kneaded.

Fingers and other objects were pushed into her open mouth as well, and a couple of times people poured wine onto her tongue and she had little alternative but to swallow.

She caught bits and pieces of the conversation around her, recognising it fairly quickly as the type of indulgent waffle one often encountered around overly educated, self-absorbed arty types.

'...The predicament of women in our modern society, where they are objectified and identified solely with their sexual...'

'...Stop the degrading portrayal of women as nothing more than a collection of body parts whose primary purpose is the sexual pleasure of men and the stimulation and titillation of ignorant...'

'...Clearly calls our minds to celebrate the sexual power of female kind and at the same time insinuates how that power can be distorted...' fingers tugged repeatedly at her nipples '...and caged by the desires of men and their cold, cruel lusts. Why, this exhibit could...'

Voices drifted away and others drifted closer. Time passed slowly for Gwen, locked in her strange little world, fingers prodding, pinching, stroking, squeezing and groping her with predictable regularity. Sometimes inquisitive fingers would rub her clitoris for a fleeting, tantalising second or two, and her traitorous juices would begin to seep. Then a finger might ease into her moist pussy and withdraw with the shameful evidence of her arousal.

After a while the touches grew more and more intermittent and the voices became fewer in number and more faint. Then, just as she was relaxing a little and least expecting it, some rascal slipped a vibrator through the hole at her pussy and began to roll it slowly up and down between her moist pussy lips, and despite her determination to defy the unfair scoundrel it took very little of this lewd attention before she was moaning helplessly through the small hole, and when a finger pushed through into her open maw she licked at it excitedly.

Then hands began to massage her buttocks, and a moment later they were pried open and she was shocked to feel a tongue circle her little puckered opening. The sensation was shockingly intimate and she trembled in her tight confines as her body began to respond with powerful reactions.

Two mouths began to work on her nipples, greedily enveloping one each. One was distinctly more eager than the other, biting and chewing and sucking as the other licked and stroked and massaged. Then the vibrator prodded her pussy lips apart and slid up inside her, pushing deep. A second vibrator began to roll back and forth across her clitoris as the first was slowly pumped in and out, and she mewled helplessly, wondering with trepidation how many people were watching the detached areas of her body being so lewdly stimulated.

The voices around her were whispers now, too faint for her to make out what they were saying. It was getting hard to think straight. The tongue circling her anus was every now and then dipping teasingly into the puckered little opening, and when it probed more forcefully her shocked system sent her into an unexpected and irresistible climax.

The sounds emerging from her open mouth were unintelligible, but she had few cares, trembling from head to toe in the anonymity of her box. Something about the isolation of the experience bored deep into her mind and she lost herself to the sensory overload, her mind turned off, rolling and spinning helplessly as the orgasm reached its peak, and then simmered, promising to return at the slightest provocation.

She was hardly aware when it all ended. She hung there dazedly, limply, not thinking, hardly realising even when the rear panel was opened and hands unstrapped and helped her out into the room. There were a dozen or so women there, all dressed expensively and fashionably. Several applauded genteelly, while others studied her with critical eyes as the maid and the redhead positioned her languorous body in front of the box.

They lifted her wrists and locked them together above her head on a hook set into the face of the box, leaving her there to recover as the gathered women deliberated and discussed her.

Gwen stood still, sagging slightly from her wrists, her body exhausted and her mind overwhelmed. It took some minutes before she could bring herself to care about the situation around her, to really notice the women - all older than she - who moved around her with such grace and style in their perfectly cut gowns and dresses.

None spoke to her or touched her now, perhaps because she was once again a person rather than merely body parts. But as she recovered she began to feel quite insignificant and uncomfortable in her nakedness. And that these women had witnessed her demeaning abuse and wanton response to it made things much worse, and she hung her head in shame, hoping hopelessly to avoid their attention.

Of course that was not going to happen. Gwen knew that all the women there were attracted to others of their own sex; they were all lesbians, or at the very least, bi-sexual. And Gwendolyn was an extremely attractive young lady who appealed to anyone with an eye for beauty and sensuality, no matter what their particular penchant. Even fully clothed, even without the intense sexuality her previous presentation had conferred upon her, there would have been many hungry looks and thoughts directed her way. As it was, naked, her slim but shapely form presented before the box that had until so recently been her prison, it was clearly all many of the sophisticated women could do to keep from taking advantage of her there and then.

After a few minutes Ms Brook swept into the room and stood next to Gwen. She had only to gesture slightly to gather the attention of all there, partly because of her authoritative persona and partly because few eyes had strayed far from Gwen since her emergence from the box.

'This is our little work of art, Gwendolyn,' she said.

The women applauded and Gwen blushed even more.

'She's a lovely young thing, of course,' Ms Brook went on whilst caressing Gwen's back with an elegant ease of movement. 'And I would like you all to note the difference between how she is being treated now as compared to when she was in the box. Now that she is recognisable as a person again, I've noticed you're all quite reluctant to touch or even approach her, even though it's been made clear to you that anyone may do so at any time. This is evidence of the dissimilarity of male and female views on the sexuality and privacy of the person. Unlike males we see the person behind the body parts - at least, when those body parts are not presented alone.'

There was more genteel applause for these words, though Gwen thought somewhat cynically of the way the women at the club had treated her. There was no great depth of respect for the privacy of her person there!

'Yet still, examine your feelings towards the sight of this lovely young creature, chained to the box, naked and vulnerable. We, as women, should feel indignation and sympathy for her plight. Yet do we? How many of you here feel only lust for her, and a desire to use her body in the tactless manner in which a man would?'

There were a few polite coughs of embarrassment and sheepish looks at her words, but one slim lady only shook her head. 'Come on, Sandra, look at her,' she said. 'Of course we feel lust for her. Who wouldn't?'

'But do you want to get to know her as a person, or do you, just as a man would, see her as a sexual object and want merely to possess her body?' Ms Brook pressed.

'I want to possess that delicious body,' someone muttered to a light ripple of laughter.

'Sexual power games aren't uniquely male,' the slim woman countered. 'Bondage and sadomasochism are not preserves of the testosterone set. You have your little April there, for one.' She pointed at the redhead, standing to one side in a very short, very tight diaphanous dress.

'That is true,' Ms Brook conceded. 'But April has given herself to me on a loving and consensual level. Gwendolyn is completely unknown to any of you except as a human masturbatory aid. You want to ravish her, to use her, to satisfy your lusts on her without regard to her needs or even who she is. And in the case of many of you she's young enough to be your own daughter.'

She smiled at Gwendolyn again, and then gestured to the maid, who moved forward and unhooked Gwen's restraints from the box, letting her arms fall.

'Let me demonstrate further,' Ms Brook continued.

April pulled a chair forward and the confident Ms Brook sat on it, then the maid positioned Gwen beside her and stepped back.

Ms Brook looked up at Gwen, and then patted her lap.

Gwen had been squirming mentally since getting out of the box, and her discomfort increased greatly when Ms Brook began talking about her, and now she felt her face turning scarlet as she realised what the woman wanted. The desire to turn and flee was almost overwhelming, yet the expectation of the many eyes upon her would not let her go. She simply could not turn and run like a timid schoolgirl.

So she shuffled forward slightly and then bent to slide her tummy over the woman's lap.

'You see how uncomfortable she is?' Ms Brook asked. 'She'd clearly rather be elsewhere, so how many of you want to see her receive a reprieve and be allowed to get up and go?'

There was an uncomfortable quiet resting over the room just as a hand rested on Gwen's upraised bottom.

'I am going to inflict considerable pain upon this vulnerable girl,' Ms Brook said. 'And, needless to say, considerable embarrassment. So does anyone here want me to send her away untouched, or are you all wanting to seeing this lovely little bottom spanked?'

Gwen felt intensely discomfited to have an audience gazing at her lying across the woman's lap, and she stared down at one leg of the chair, trying to pretend the women were not there, watching.

Then she gasped as Ms Brook slapped her bottom. It stung, and in the sting she could feel the echo of the strapping the hateful Carol had given her not so long before.

Another very hard blow made her jerk and she bit her lip at the stinging pain that speared through her body.

'See the violation of perfection,' Ms Brook said. 'The unmarred ivory skin now marked by the violence of objectification and avaricious lust.'

Another blow landed, and another, and Gwen writhed with each strike, her bottom starting to grow painfully hot. The pain mounted as the blows continued, then grew even more terrible as Ms Brook switched to a round wooden paddle handed to her by the ever-attentive maid. The sound of the blows landing on her bare skin echoed throughout the room, accompanied by her yelps and cries as she squirmed on the immovable lap and fought to keep the tears from spilling from her eyes.

Her bottom hurt terribly, and each new blow made her more and more desperate to avoid another. Yet she could not bring herself to beg; not where so many others would witness her weakness. Her body shuddered to her suppressed sobs, and she twisted more and more desperately so Ms Brook had to hold her even more firmly in place.

Then Gwen was abruptly dumped on the floor, and before she could gather her spiralling thoughts Ms Brook stood and grabbed her by the hair and tugged her up to her knees, forcing her head back so that the assembled women could gaze upon her tears.

'And you all love it,' Ms Brook said. 'For that is what we are; a predatory species. We prey on that which rouses our hungers, and yearn to conquer and see it conquered. We don't merely want to join with this lovely morsel of flesh in a mutually pleasurable act, we want to use her, to ravish her body and mind and soul. Her degradation arouses and excites us because it gives us the thought that any one of us could use her howsoever we choose.'

She twisted Gwen's hair back more sharply and the girl cried out, defensively reaching up and back only to have her wrists pinned together there in a firm grip, forcing her to arch back for the watching throng.

'How many of you feel sorry for her, as opposed to wanting to get your greedy hands on her?' Ms Brook asked with an arrogant, knowing smirk. 'How many want to beat her and dominate her, to force her to satisfy your lusts? What force and violence would we subject her lovely young flesh to in order to satisfy ourselves of our superiority, to degrade her to the point of servitude?'

She ran a controlling hand over Gwen's body, squeezing her breasts, then pushed her forward and released her wrists. Gwen fell onto her hands and the maid, yet again responding to an unspoken command from her mistress, stepped forward and removed the chair.

'A final abject lesson in objectification and the power of sexual lust,' Ms Brook concluded.

There were gasps and murmurs from the assembled women, and Gwen looked up from the floor through her tousled fringe to see a new person approaching her. The women drew back en masse, many looking indignant and displeased.

It was a man, incredibly muscular and naked but for a loincloth.

'Do we, as lesbians, feel appalled at the prospect of this lovely but helpless girl being ravaged by an ox-like male?' Ms Brook's voice invaded the tense atmosphere. 'Or do we feel continuing, perhaps even expanded arousal at the thought of her being so degraded?'

Gwen was stunned, not quite sure what was now evolving.

The man moved behind her, and then dropped his loincloth. He was semi-erect, and as his penis lifted and blossomed before Gwen's spellbound face the women pulled extravagant faces of distaste.

Gwen gawped at him, the blood draining from her face as she realised Ms Brook intended him to use her right there in front of all the gathered women. She started to rise but he dropped to his knees and shoved her back down, then roughly spread her legs, gripping the back of her neck with a firm hand to hold her in place.

'W-wait...' she pleaded quietly. 'Not here... not in front of *them*...'

She had already been so thoroughly degraded in front of the sophisticated women that the thought of being used by a male, which they would no doubt consider the ultimate in degradation, made her desperate to avoid him. Yet in her weakened and dazed state her resistance was uncoordinated and uncertain and he easily held her in place as Ms Brook's voice overrode her pleas.

'Examine your own emotions at the present time,' Ms Brook instructed her guests. 'Perhaps politically, perhaps intellectually, you feel the urge to rush forward to save this girl from the rough and brutal violation at the hands of this bull of a creature. But what are we feeling emotionally? What do our loins say? Are we not even now eagerly awaiting the moment of her violation, wanting to watch this beautiful female being mounted?'

Gwen cried out weakly as the man slapped her red bottom, and he laughed, reaching round to roughly squeeze her breasts. Then she felt his erection prodding at her sex. She was panting heavily, disbelief filling her frantic mind, and then felt the insistent demand for entry increase. Her swollen sex lips were eased aside, and then his steel hard column of flesh drove deep into her body with a single, powerful thrust.

'Ungghhhh!' Her cry echoed about the room, but there was little sympathy in the eyes of the spectators. Their faces were flushed with excitement and the sight captivated their eyes as the powerful man plunged into her from behind and then ground his groin against her sore bottom.

His hands held her waist just above her hips. He drew his erection back, and then thrust in once more as aggressively as before. Her head jerked up and back, her hair swaying and curtaining her face, yet he held her easily in place, slowly drawing his stiff lance back until only the head remained between her labia, then driving it into her once again, using it like a spear, stabbing her with its lust and strength and fury.

Gwen instinctively began to jerk her hips back to meet him then, and the force of his penetrations doubled. His cock sliced through the soft folds of her sex with cruel, powerful forays. He rode her; rode her with more power and technique than even Richardson had done, for he had more of both. There, on all fours amid the silent circle of women she was ridden with lust and overwhelming authority, his strong hands occasionally roving around her soft form to maul her breasts or pull back on her hair.

And yet, despite the mortification she experienced, she also felt a small but growing sense of elation - of freedom. She was outside societal rules and requirements. She was not a part of these women but an abject lesson to them. She was a creature, a thing, an example of uncontrolled sexual lust, and that masochistic side of her that Richardson had been bringing to the surface basked in her abuse, in being the centre of attention.

The shocked revulsion in the faces of the watching lesbians could not hide the heat and desire in their eyes as they stared, spellbound, at her ravishment, wishing it were them behind her, using her, mounting her, thrusting into her so cruelly and vigorously.

The pleasure grew along with that sense of sexual abandon, blotting out her embarrassment and appealing to that dark side of her that Richardson had discovered. But the climax, when it came, was brief, for her mind and body were too worn out - too exhausted.

And there was no time to build up into something more powerful either, for his use of her was too wild and uncontrolled and could not be sustained past a very few minutes. Soon he was coming inside her, grunting his pleasure to the appalled yet captivated audience, letting his seed flow into her belly as he slowly halted his rutting strokes and then casually withdrew.

The redhead, April, helped Gwen to her feet and then led her silently out of the room, up the stairs, and back to the sanctuary of the bedroom.

Chapter 12

'How do you feel?' April asked with apparently genuine concern. 'Jeez, he was rough! You must ache all over!'

'I... I'm all right,' Gwen told her.

'Ms Brook paddled you something fierce, too,' the girl said sympathetically. 'Your poor bottom. Come with me.'

She led Gwen into the adjoining bathroom where a large marble tub had already been filled with steaming water, then stripped and stepped into it with Gwen, hugging her and whispering comfortingly.

Gwen found that extremely calming and reassuring after the strange and shocking emotional turbulence she had experienced earlier.

'Are you and Ms Brook lovers?' she asked abruptly.

'Ms Brook?' The girl chuckled sweetly. 'No, she's my mistress. I'm her slave.'

'Her slave?'

'Uhuh,' the girl smiled coyly and nodded as she spoke, 'her sex slave. And you belong to Mr Richardson, don't you?' she asked.

Gwen was slightly startled at the suggestion. 'Belong?' she echoed, slightly aghast. 'No. I mean, I'm staying with him at the moment and um, we ah... we...'

'He ties you up and uses you, and chastises you when you're disobedient?' the redhead finished for her.

'Well, I um,' Gwen struggled to find a suitable reply, 'I suppose so, but...'

'But you can't disobey him no matter what he orders you to do?'

'I can leave,' Gwen said doubtfully, finding the astuteness of the girl somewhat unsettling. Was she really so transparent?

'Of course you can. And I can leave Ms Brook as well. But while I'm with her I am her slave and she can do anything she wants with me or give me to anyone she wants.'

'But I'm not a slave,' Gwen retorted indignantly.

'Of course you are, darling,' April chuckled. 'You're just not calling it that. I mean, did he ask you before sending you with Carol to the club? Did he ask you before agreeing to loan you to Ms Brook? Nobody asks a slave what she wants to do. They just have her do it.'

A slave?

Gwen tried to wrap her mind around the concept. Despite the fact that she had given herself to Richardson and let him use and punish her as he chose she had not considered their relationship in quite that light. Perhaps because she was still young enough to recall being spanked for childhood misdeeds and because he was old enough to be her father she had put their relationship, however sexual, in terms with which she was more familiar, such as a student and her tutor; she must, of course, obey or be punished.

And yet she felt a sudden deep realisation that her relationship with Richardson really was that of a master and his slave. He had used the word servant, perhaps not wanting to frighten her, but he was using her, treating her, and punishing her as a slave!

She *was* a sex slave!

The idea was mesmerising and something seemed to click within her as if her mind almost instantly adjusted to and accepted such a role for her. With it came a low throbbing between her legs as her mind raced through the things she had experienced over the past few days and the abuse she had been subjected to.

'You've never been a sex slave before, have you?' the lovely redhead pressed.

Gwen shook her head.

'I was a sex slave to another woman before Ms Brook,' April went on airily. 'I gave myself to her when I was a teenager and was her slave for three years. Then she gave me to Ms Brook when I turned twenty-one. Ms Brook is sterner, but she cares more for me. My previous mistress, I think, was more enthusiastic about dominating my body than loving me as a person. Do you think Richardson loves you?'

'Oh, heavens no!' Gwen exclaimed.

'Why did you give yourself to him, then? Just for the sexual excitement? There are tons and tons of nicer men who would love to have a slave like you, and a lot of them are wealthy too. For that matter you could make a fortune with one of those elite escort agencies that specialise in bondage. I hear that on average the girls get more than a thousand dollars a night.'

'I - I never really thought about it,' Gwen admitted.

Had she given herself to Richardson? Well, she supposed she had, in a way. But she was hardly inclined to tell April she had done so in exchange for room and board. That was simply too pathetic.

Besides, that was not the entirety of it. She was simply bored. That had always been her problem. That had been why she jetted off to America to begin with. And being around Richardson, having him do such wicked sexual things to her, well, it was certainly not boring. Rather, she felt more alive than she ever had before, with one shocking new experience following another.

April smiled softly and kissed her on the cheek, and Gwen turned without thinking and kissed her back, on the lips. April giggled a little and snuggled in more closely. Her hand slipped down between Gwen's legs and her fingers gently caressed her sex lips. 'And you've been well and truly fucked, haven't you?' she whispered bluntly.

Gwen nodded.

'And you like it? That's a part of being a slave, to enjoy being overcome and ravished.' She stood up and held her hands down to Gwen, who took them somewhat shyly and stepped out of the fragrant water.

April helped dry her, and then had her bend over while she spread a soothing balm across her thighs and buttocks. She brushed and dried her hair, then led her back to the bedroom and climbed into bed with her.

She lay half atop Gwen's body, kissing her gently as Gwen responded, and their hands moved slowly over one another as April gradually slipped further over her body.

'Spread your legs,' she urged in hushed tones. 'Further...'

Gwen parted her thighs and April angled her pelvis, spreading her own legs until their pussies could press gently together. It was a gentle lovemaking, like nothing Gwen had experienced of late. The girl's body was silky and warm, and felt quite delicious against her own.

Their hands caressed, exploring one another's bodies, and their hips moved in slow, rhythmic motion.

Each had savoured a gentle yet fulfilling orgasm, and Gwen was beginning to develop real feelings for April when the door opened, throwing a stream of light across the bed. Her initial reaction was to gasp in shock and embarrassment, but she was oddly confused to realise there was much less of the latter than she would have expected. Certainly April showed no sign of shame at being interrupted.

'Yes, mistress?' she asked simply, squinting towards the shard of light and the shadow framed there.

Ms Brook moved into the room, frowning, hands clasping a good deal of leather gear which she dropped on the bed. April sat up obediently while Gwen fought off the feeling of a teenager caught necking by her parents.

'Richardson wants her back immediately,' Ms Brook announced. 'Prepare her for travel, April, and hurry.'

'Yes, mistress,' April said, sliding elegantly out of bed.

Ms Brook examined Gwen closely, her eyes roaming over her body, then turned and left without another word.

'I guess we'd better get you ready to go,' April said, picking up a leather strap and examining it.

'I suppose so,' Gwen said, feeling confused and reluctant. Why should she have to go anywhere just because Richardson wanted her to? She had been enjoying herself, and found herself growing resentful at being interrupted by the man. She really was going to have to tell him off and set him straight quite soon.

'Stand up,' April said.

Gwen considered refusing, but April was only doing what Ms Brook ordered, so she sighed and climbed out of bed, and then turned at April's direction.

Her wrists were strapped together behind her back, and while she felt a sense of annoyance as it was done this very quickly and surprisingly passed into one of renewed arousal. She pulled against the strap, feeling a little thrum of excitement between her legs as she was once again returned to a state of helplessness.

'What's this?' she asked, eyeing the strange harness affair April was sliding over her head.

'It's better than having a nasty old ball-gag in your mouth,' April replied.

The straps fitted over her head and then the thing was pulled tight, a chinstrap clamping her mouth firmly closed. April then had her lay on the bed and bent her left leg back, pushing her bare foot up against her buttock. She then slipped a strap around her thigh and tugged it tight, binding her leg up and back. She did the same with her right leg, then put restraints around her ankles and snapped them together. Another strap was attached to the one around her wrists and April pulled.

Gwen grunted as her body was bent back farther and farther, and tried to open her mouth to complain, but she couldn't, and her wrists were soon strapped tightly to her ankles. Another strap was attached to the harness around her head and pulled even more tightly back, straining her like a taut bow.

She then heard the detestable Carol's voice, and then strong hands picked her up and carried her out of the bedroom, down the stairs and out to the garage. She was placed in the boot of another car and the top slammed shut. Moments later the car was in motion, heading, she presumed, for Richardson.

Though, of course, she could not know that. How strange, she thought, to let oneself be so completely at the mercy of others. She had never been asked if she wanted to be given to a horde of lesbians to be a plaything, yet had not been given the opportunity to protest until her gag was removed at the club, and by then she was too lost to it all to really do so.

Nor had she been consulted about becoming a public spectacle and art piece. Yet she'd had the opportunity to protest after arriving, and had not - not even when it was obvious she was to be fucked by the muscled man in front of all those despicable women. She had been appalled, or at least a part of her had been appalled, yet she made little effort to resist.

Why?

What on earth was becoming of her that she made no protest to such things? Not too long ago she had been a feisty character who would have been outraged had someone even presumed to order her food or drink in a restaurant without consulting her, yet now a man she barely knew gave her to strangers for their perverse gratification and she said nothing by way of complaint.

And how much did she enjoy it? a smug inner voice asked.

Gwen grunted as the car hit a pothole and she banged her temple. Her poor trussed body was aching more fiercely with every passing minute. Why must she be bound so tightly? Did they think she would break free and run? Clearly she could not.

And what day was it?

She yawned, and then felt her stomach rumble. She had gotten little sleep and not much to eat since arriving at Richardson's penthouse; somewhat ironic given her desire for a warm bed and decent food had led her to him in the first place.

Despite her sore back she almost dozed off a few times during the cramped journey, but some bump or turn always brought her back to groggy wakefulness.

Then the car stopped and the boot opened and Carol was lifting her out and carrying her to the elevator. She set her on the floor and then backed out, leaving her alone as the doors smoothed shut. The lift rose on its own, and she stared at the corner near the ceiling, wondering if he were watching her at that moment.

The doors opened and Richardson gazed down at her, a look of smug satisfaction on his face.

'Don't want to have anything to do with lesbians, hmm?' he asked acidly. 'I understand you enjoyed yourself thoroughly.'

He bent over her, undoing the strap holding her head back and she groaned with relief as her neck muscles relaxed. He then removed the strap holding her ankles and wrists together, and she let out a long moan of sheer bliss as the pressure on her spine dissipated.

Hanging upside down in the dark was not conducive to clear thinking, especially as Gwen was already exhausted. She spent the first few minutes massaging her neck and knees, the latter being difficult to accomplish as she had to raise herself, and her back was really not in the mood for stressful work. With her wrists bound in front of her, however, she could do little things like scratch her nose when it itched, and she was unreasonably grateful for this.

The night passed in a dark haze. Her head ached and after a while it was hard to tell up from down. Occasionally she fell asleep, only to wake in confusion and disorientation. A soft voice whispered in the background of pleasure and obedience, but she could barely hear it and had no idea if it was even real.

The lights woke her as they flickered on, and she was confused through her headache to see the room was upside down. She blinked at it but it failed to change about. She was lowered to the floor and lay limp, staring at the ceiling, feeling extremely light-headed.

While she lay there Richardson produced a pair of leather sleeves. He bent her legs back one at a time, as they had been the previous evening, and then slid one sleeve up past her knees. It grew tighter as he tugged it up, and in the end had her feet jammed back against her thighs.

'Wha... what are you doing?' she asked fearfully.

He produced a pair of odd leather mittens and pulled them on over her hands. They had no fingers, not even thumbs, and her hands were forced into fists as he tugged them down around her wrists and then buckled them in place. Then the other sleeve was placed around her arms, cocooning them tightly.

'Stop it,' she said feebly.

A moment later her hair, in a loose ponytail, was lifted and pulled through a coin-sized opening in the top of a leather hood, which he smoothed over her head.

'I'm thirsty,' she complained. 'And I'm hungry.'

Richardson ignored her, and the hood was tightened beneath her chin. There were no eyeholes and she was cut off from her surroundings as a collar slipped around her throat, then two determined fingers pinched in at the sides of her cheeks, forcing her mouth open. Something was then carefully placed inside - a plastic ring of sorts that kept her mouth open.

Now her protests were mere whimpers and faint grunts, and she made more of them as pain bit her nipples, even while recognising the clips that bit into her tender flesh. Strong hands flipped her onto all fours, on her elbows and knees. Then she felt something between her buttocks, probing her anus, and a small ball was pushed inside. Her sphincter closed behind it, cosseting the intruder snugly. Something long and soft was now protruding from between her buttocks, and as she moved a fraction what felt like a main of hair brushed against her thighs.

A small clip was fastened to her clitoris, but it was quite weak in comparison to those dangling from her nipples, and provided only mild discomfort.

'Come, we'll get you something to drink,' she heard, and felt a surge of relief as he guided her by the leash he had attached to her collar. She crawled blindly, turning as the leash pulled, halting when he directed.

'There's a bowl of water right in front of you,' Richardson said.

She lowered her head, her lips searching, and knocked against the side of the bowl. Her chin plunged into the cool liquid and she used her tongue catlike to quench her thirst.

That need satisfied, her stomach rumbled demandingly and she raised her head blindly.

'Want something to eat, do you?' he goaded. Gwen nodded enthusiastically.

'But how do you expect to eat when you can't chew?'

She had no answer to that, her mind not quite up to solving problems yet, but Richardson solved it by feeding her a thin but tasty soup through a straw.

Once replenished the leash guided her again, and she guessed they had returned to the little torture room.

'Back up a little,' Richardson ordered, and she obeyed, her vulnerable pussy making contact with something she quickly recognised as a vibrator. The nose of it rested lightly just within her, and she felt its intense vibrations beginning to excite her.

'I'll be back,' he said, and left her alone once again.

Gwen tested her bonds experimentally. She had no hands with which to undo buckles or snaps. She tried crawling a little way forward but yelped and backed up instantly; it seemed he had fastened the chain attached to her clitoris clip to something behind her.

She could, however, move backwards a little, sliding her pussy slowly down the length of the vibrator until it was buried inside her. The vibrator was oddly shaped, having a smaller round nub pushing down and forward near its base so as to press directly against her clitoris. Despite her predicament she ground herself against it experimentally, and then with growing excitement as it set her clitoris pulsing deliciously.

What was there to think about but base animal instincts, after all? Nothing else seemed to matter any more. Food, water, pleasure. What else was worth thinking about? What else could she have?

She ground herself wantonly against it, slowly riding back and forth along the length of the thing, her mind thinking only of the pleasure filling her body as she trembled and sighed.

So tired was she that she came quietly, sighing blissfully through the strange gag, her insides melting as she sagged weakly while the orgasm faded...

Why was she there, naked and chained like an animal, degrading herself and waiting for Richardson to return and degrade her further?

A sound made her flinch just as a hand slipped between her legs, and a moment later she felt pressure on her collar.

'Come,' Richardson ordered.

Gwen eased forward carefully but found herself no longer chained in place, and followed him again on her elbows and knees.

'Keep that backside high,' he instructed as they moved, his requirements accompanied by a sharp stinging snap of a strap across her buttocks that made her yelp.

She heard the murmur of voices ahead and they turned, then went down a step into what she knew was the front room.

'Hell!' a male voice exclaimed. 'You really know how to keep your women in their place, don't you?'

'Certain types of women,' Richardson replied.

'Lovely body...' another voice enthused, and beneath the hood Gwen blushed furiously with embarrassment and excitement. She was grateful to the hood for the element of anonymity, and for preventing her from seeing their eyes. And then she gasped as a male hand groped her breasts.

'Very nice,' a voice said, close by.

She thought there were three of them, not counting Richardson, but could only identify them when they spoke.

Gwen knew she was a sex slave. But the words were strangely comforting, somehow easing her humiliation and rousing the fire in her belly. Yes, she was a sex slave to the despicable men, their helpless prisoner, unable to resist their filthy desires and lusts. She formed that image in her mind and felt the heat grow, felt herself begin to exult in the demeaning and degrading words they spat at her.

'You're asking too low a price,' she heard, and then her collar was tugged and she crawled forward, around in a slow circle, and then another swipe on her bottom from the strap made her jerk sharply.

'Keep that ass high,' Richardson ordered.

'Nice tail on her,' someone commented.

Fingers pushed into her sex, first two, then three, and a hand slapped her bottom.

'Spread them wider,' a coarse voice ordered.

Someone then gripped her ponytail, using it to force her head up and back, and she felt the spongy warmth of a man's cock pushing through the ring that held her mouth open and sliding across her tongue. It pumped in and out a few times then thrust smoothly into her throat. Hands groped her breasts, roughly pinching her nipples and tugging on the weights.

Whoever was behind her tired of merely using his fingers and thrust his erection into her with a masculine grunt of satisfaction. She felt him penetrate the soft moist folds of her sex to drive deeply into her.

Hands gripped her hips, holding her steady as a hairy groin pummelled her bottom, agitating the ball lodged just inside her rear passage. Then the stranger eased back and pulled her to meet his next flurry of thrusts.

Meanwhile the cock in her throat was pumping rapidly in and out, the hand gripping her hair tugging as if to emphasise the man's power over her, while a hand she presumed was his roughly mauled her breasts.

She caught snatches of sneering conversation between them, but her mind was failing to really grasp the meaning of their words.

Words weren't really important - not unless they were commands...

Chapter 13

The man was Japanese. He was stout and white-haired, and fairly old.

Gwen did not know who he was or his name. He had entered the room alone, smiling down at her as she lay in the cage, then unlocked it and ordered her out in a surprisingly gentle voice. He removed the leather restraints around her wrists and ankles, brushing her hair back from her face with his fingers as he smiled down at her.

The ropes he held were quite thick, but soft and flexible.

He smiled as he saw her eyes moving anxiously over the long lengths. 'Rope,' he said, and when she looked up at him he smiled. 'Rope is what a true artist works with. Rope can be shaped by a true artist's imagination.'

He took her wrist and carefully looped the rope around it several times. She watched as he laid each one perfectly alongside the next until six neat loops were wrapped around her slender wrist. He turned her gently, a single finger pressed against her shoulder, and lifted her arm up behind her, raising it higher and higher until she gasped with discomfort. He lowered it then, his fingers kneading and massaging her shoulder and upper arm, then began to raise it in slow, gentle pumping motions until her quivering fingers were almost touching the back of her neck.

He brought the rope over her shoulder and down between her breasts, looping it back up beneath her right breast then around the other side, drawing it back over her shoulder again. Lifting her other wrist up, he again worked it higher and higher then tied it in place and brought the rope across her other shoulder. As before it looped up beneath and around her left breast, so that now both were somewhat constricted. The rope returned over her shoulder and dropped down her back, then he began to massage her shoulders once again, and drew the rope around her arms and bent to force her elbows back together.

This was more difficult, but he was patient, and her hurting did not seem to bother him. He shushed her and cooed gently as he slowly forced them together, then looped the rope twice around her front, once just above her breasts pushing down, and once just below pushing up.

He tied the loops off behind her then let the rope drop down between her buttocks. A deft hand reached between her legs and pulled it through, then up to her belly. There a finger held it in place while the rope slipped sideways around her waist, then returned to tie off. It circled her waist again, then dropped between her legs and pulled up tight, then tighter, then agonisingly tight, digging between her labia and crushing up into her sex, grinding against her clitoris as he tied the loops off behind her.

Double loops slipped around her thighs, knees and calves and ankles in a figure eight pattern, binding her legs tightly together. Then smaller vertical loops pinched each of them tight.

Finally, apparently pleased, he stepped back to admire his work.

'Simple, but effective, until we get to my place,' he mused, with a sparkle in his eyes.

Another rope went over her head then down beneath her jaw, pulling tight. It circled several times, then twisted and went horizontally around her head, over her eyes so that she could not see, and then over her mouth, prising between her lips.

She heard him say, 'Take her,' and was lifted across someone's shoulder, then carried out of the room. Eventually she sensed rather than heard the hush of the sliding doors, and then felt the lift sinking. The cold outside air kissed her skin, then warmth enveloped it again as she was placed into a vehicle of some kind.

During the short journey she heard his voice again, talking to someone, and then she was lifted out of the car and carried down a flight of steps. Then she was settled down on some kind of soft rug.

'Now we have more time,' she heard him say.

The loops of rope were slowly and carefully removed from her body, starting with those around her head. She was in a room with a low ceiling, stone walls and no windows. There were several squat tables and sturdy chairs set about, as well as a pair of large chests and an antique desk.

He laid her back on one of the low tables and began to ensnare her with rope once again. This time he used different thicknesses and meticulously laid the rope in an intertwining pattern of circles and loops that constricted her flesh. Her breasts were encircled carefully, the man paying great care to squeeze them to the exact degree of firmness. Then much thinner cord crossed her breasts, going from one side to the other, then back again. He plucked at her nipples, and then twisted the thin cord in tightly so that the erect pink buds were caught between the two taut cords.

Two more cords crossed vertically, again pressing in together against the sides of her nipples. He spent a great deal of time, loosening and tightening until perfectly satisfied all was as he wanted it.

The rope was fed down between her legs once more, and then he tied a thin length of cord to its end.

'Hyzala fibre,' he whispered. 'From the jungles of Paraguay. Very resilient - very elastic.'

Gwen had yet to say anything. It seemed she had fallen out of the habit of speaking, for some reason. She had spent several days on her knees and elbows at the mercy of others, only really allowed to speak when spoken to, and punished whenever she spoke without being given permission. During that time she had been used by many, often spanked or switched before others. She had grown used to keeping her eyes submissively downcast, unwilling to meet their looks of contempt, and keeping her mouth shut.

The man tied a small loop in the chord as he laid it along her body, and his fingers spread her pussy open, easing aside her tender clitoris. His fingers stroked her there as he cooed, and her clit began to swell with desire. Then the loop was slipped around it and tightened before he pulled the cord down and up between her buttocks. There it met another loop of rope, which travelled up the length of her back to tie up around her shoulders.

He eased her off the table and onto her feet, then smiled as he had her straighten up, and then smiled anew as she gasped and bent forward to try to ease the discomfort, then he reached behind her, seizing her hair and pulling, the vicious tug on her scalp forcing her to straighten again and the ropes dug into her shoulders, into her pussy, and pulled the elastic cord around her clitoris even tighter.

'Owww...' she wailed miserably.

'Only a little pinching,' he said, smiling. 'You English girls - you are supposed to have the stiff upper lip, is that not so?'

'It h-hurts!' she gasped.

'Yes, but only a little bit,' he mused. 'A little pinch is all. You are an English lady; you must preserve face, show no reaction.'

English lady?

Yes, of course she was. She shook her fuzzy head. It was hard to remember very much beyond... before... Images flittered behind her eyes and she wondered vaguely what she was doing there.

The white-haired man fussed over her for several more minutes, then examined her, apparently very pleased with her and his handiwork.

And then, for some bizarre reason Gwen could not understand, he untied her completely and began to tie her up once again.

'I was in London recently,' he said as though holding a perfectly normal conversation in perfectly normal circumstances. 'I shopped in Bond Street and bought a nice suit there. I went on a boat on the Thames. It is a lovely city. Have you ever been there...?'

Had Gwendolyn Allison Pepperdine ever been to London? Who was this silly old man? Of course she had been to London! She practically lived there!

'...I stayed at a top hotel. They have a lovely restaurant there. It was cool but not nearly so cold as New York, and there was no snow. There was a lovely...'

He droned on about London as he bound her, and her hazy mind provided images to match the descriptions he gave.

Soon she was hanging in mid-air, held horizontally in a virtual net of interlinked rope loops, her legs lifted high, her big toes bound by narrow cords cut to length to apply a precise degree of pull, her arms lifted up and back, thumbs aching from their own separate bondage, breasts hanging, plucked by cords. Her hair had been wound into a careful tail and then circled along its entire length by carefully laid loops of twine that pulled her head up.

He left her like that for a while as he cut more cord, twine and rope to measure, chatting softly all the while about England and restaurants and theatres and hotels and shops, as well as an English butler he had hired at some mansion or other he owned.

The divergence between the images that sprang unbidden to her mind and her present situation became more and more of a contrast as time passed. And her mind, which seemed to have been asleep for some days, was beginning to puzzle at why she was allowing herself to be subjected to such levels of discomfort and abuse without question or protest.

He lowered her to the floor, untied her, and then retied her once more. This time the ropes formed a diamond pattern in her pale skin as they interlaced across her torso. A length of bamboo was placed behind her knees and her legs then bent back and tied in place. She was lifted into the air again, this time upside down, hanging from the bamboo pole.

Her arms were bound behind her back with another length of bamboo under them. Her wrists were fastened tightly to a length of cord that was laid down between her buttocks, up between her sex lips, then around her hips, pulling in tightly. A large knot in the cord was placed right over her clitoris. Weights were then placed on the lower pole to put more and more pressure on her body, which soon began to feel as though it would tear apart under the strain. The backs of her legs screamed where they were bent over the top pole and the bottom pole was digging into her armpits.

As a final touch her hair, still tightly bound in twine, was pulled up and back and bound to a wooden peg pushed into her anus.

As before the man spent several minutes admiring his work, moving around her, muttering to himself and nodding his head. Then he sat and began to cut more rope and twine for some new purpose.

When he was done he set her down once more, untied her, and began anew. This time he hung two long lengths of rope from the ceiling and stood her on a low stool. He raised her arms and then carefully entwined each one with snakelike curls descending from wrist to shoulder. The two loops then slipped around her chest above and below her breasts, with a tight layer between the two to draw the loops closed.

Thin twine made an X across each breast, the centre of which was a small tight loop binding each aching nipple. Two more loops of rope descended down the centre of her body front and back, passing between her legs. Twine encircled her hips, and then pulled down carefully between her legs, a loop ensnaring her clitoris and closing tightly. Then the rope passed over it and was tied tightly between her legs, again with a large knot just over her clitoris.

He removed the stool then, and her weight fell upon the rope. Some of that weight was on her arms and chest, and she felt the ropes digging painfully into her tender breasts as well. But most was on the two loops which prised her pussy lips apart and met beneath her, and the pressure of that was fairly agonising.

Of course, he was not yet finished. First he carefully bound her legs together in an interlaced pattern that kept her from twitching so much as a toe. After admiring that for a time he unbound her legs, spread them wide, then laid separate winding layers of rope down their length to the ankles, fed the ropes through rings in a pair of beams, and hung gradually increasing weights from them.

The pain was now intense, and her cries and sobs were met with a curious smile as he admired his handiwork. Her pussy was on fire, the discomfort worse than anything she had yet experienced, yet there was a subversive element of arousal accompanying it, and that element had been present for as long as she could remember being with Richardson or his acquaintances. But it was not strong enough for her to fight through the growing torment between her legs.

She demanded her release, demanded he cut her down, cursed him until he tied another rough rope around her head, with a large knot positioned to block her mouth much as the rubber ball-gags Richardson had used.

But the treatment she was receiving brought an anger she had not felt for some time, and the anger was like a hot fire licking away the cobwebs that had been gathering in her mind. For the first time since putting herself in Richardson's hands she felt herself an unwilling prisoner - for real. The smiling old man and the pain of her bondage evoked her rage in a way Richardson and others never had. His complete indifference to her suffering, the fact that he was so obviously interested in her only as a *thing*, as an object, as a model to lay his designs upon, raised her indignation to a mighty fury, and she strained helplessly against the ropes biting into her flesh as she sought to free herself.

Of course she could not and exhausted herself very quickly, soon hanging limp, sobbing weakly at the discomfort and ignominy of it all. The old man left the room, muttering, and the pain slowly faded to a dull throb.

He returned after a while and removed the weights from her feet, then untied them and left once more, still muttering to himself.

The pressure was now not nearly as bad. Her pussy still ached yet the sense of relief was tremendous. She hung still for some time, waiting for the old man to return, and gradually her body began to detect a small but delicious little sense of pleasure coming from her groin. Her legs shifted fractionally and she winced as the ropes nibbled at her sex. Yet the additional pressure brought only a little more pain - along with a considerable rise in pleasure.

Her legs felt leaden, like dead weights. But she slowly moved her right one forward and her left back - just a bit - and shuddered as the knot over her clitoris shifted. It was almost like sandpaper against her sensitive nubbin, yet the sensation of pleasure was intoxicating. She groaned weakly and shifted her legs back, shuddering with the delicious wave of pleasure that streamed through her veins.

She arched her back and the ropes around her breasts tightened, and her nipples throbbed within the tight confines of twine encircling them. She shifted her legs again, trembling as the twine dug into her clitoris, squeezing it tightly, and the larger knot of rope ground against it from above. The pain was more intense with her more energetic movement, but the pleasure was overwhelming. Her nether parts had never been so sensitive; been so deeply, darkly stimulated.

She scissored her legs, crying out with the turmoil the movement created, then stiffening and shaking violently as convulsions rippled along her spine. Her head jerked and her body shook and writhed in the ropes as the climax gripped her, and her own uncontrolled movements served to heighten the stimulation of her body as the ropes pulled and pinched and twisted.

Gwen collapsed, gulping in air, perspiring heavily, yet still pulsing with dreamy delight. Her lower body began to undulate, her legs swinging together, forward and back, forward and back, sawing her pussy against the rope digging into her sensitive flesh. She came again, crying out in rapturous pleasure, the burning heat of pain subdued by a torrent of white-hot ecstasy.

She was burning up. She was being cut in half. She was dying. But only the pleasure mattered. Only clinging to that pleasure for another few seconds, then another few, then just a few more held any meaning at all.

She hung limp again, chest and belly aching from the terrible spasming of muscles. She whimpered, her head hanging back, jaw slack, and hissed as her back arched and her nipples pulled against the twine holding them. Her breasts strained against the rope digging into them, and then her lower body began to undulate once more.

When the old man returned and cut her down she was in no state of mind to complain or demand she be released. Limp and exhausted she was bound artfully in rope, with a large knot pushed into her mouth, and then carried back to the car. She was in a daze most of the trip, then carried up to the luxury apartment and placed in her cage. She was sat back against the bars and her arms were shackled. Then her legs were lifted up and back and also shackled at both knees, and she was left alone.

Gwen noticed, as she had not for some days, the words softly proclaiming the joy of submission and the need to please her master, and this time felt a small wave of resentment before drifting off to sleep.

She woke as was normal, to find Richardson opening her cage. He released her from her shackles and she groaned as she sprawled weakly on the floor, body stiff and aching, but the snap of his switch soon had her on all fours as he leashed her and led her crawling along the hall. He was annoyed with her because the rope had left red marks on her flesh, especially one running between her buttocks and up her abdomen.

And she felt sore, especially between the legs. She vaguely recalled the old man rubbing some sort of cream into her there, but she still hurt. She did not try to ignore that pain but instead clung to it; it cleared her mind somewhat, so that even while she carried on her morning duties instinctively her mind sat apart, frowning in suspicion and disapproval as she licked at his shoes, ate her food and drank her water from bowls on the floor, knelt calmly as he buggered her - even feeling grateful to him for not penetrating her aching pussy - then knelt meekly as he informed her of her duties for the day.

She was to sweep every rug and wash every floor. She would do this while crawling on all fours, of course, using a pail and scrubbing brush.

He showered and shaved, then prepared to leave. But before going he sat on one of the sturdy antique chairs and ordered her to place herself across his lap. Naked, she felt the smooth texture of his expensive clothing against her flesh as she obeyed, and her mind felt another little burst of resentment and disapproval.

Then he spanked her, punishing her for the marks on her skin, marks which were none of her doing. The unfairness of that did not penetrate at first; she had, of late, come to accept punishment with or without cause as her just reward for...

For what, she could not quite remember. But regardless of cause Richardson's hand struck firmly and painfully as it ranged up and down her buttocks, turning them a bright pink, then an angry red that matched the welts the ropes had left.

When done he strapped her ankles back to her thighs, securing the straps in place with small padlocks, then left her to her work, apparently confident she would do it.

What a rat he was!

It had only been a few days... or had it? It occurred to Gwen just then that she could not quite recall how many days she had been with Richardson. One day seemed to run into another, with nothing to mark the borders between them. Sometimes she was placed in the cage to sleep, but not at any precisely set time. Sometimes she spent hours in the cage, sometimes hanging by her ankles, sometimes manipulated into uncomfortable positions. She could not tell noon from midnight except from looking out of the windows - when she was not blindfolded or in the torture chamber.

She crawled towards the closet where the buckets and cleaning equipment were kept, then halted, annoyed at herself for her automatic obedience to his word. She reached back and rubbed her tender behind, then eased a finger between her legs, gasping as she touched her tender clitoris.

She changed direction, wary as she did so, for doing anything against his specific orders inevitably drew punishment. But she went into his bedroom and then into the toilet, where she looked up at the medicine cabinet. On her knees reaching it seemed an insurmountable difficulty, and she had, of late, gotten into the habit of accepting rather than solving problems.

Still, she went to the corner and dragged over a chair, then hauled herself up onto it, and from there crawled unsteadily up onto the wide counter. From there she reached up and opened the cabinet, searching for medicines. She found some aspirin and a cream of lotion for scrapes, cuts and burns. Pleased with herself she turned on the faucet and swallowed a couple of pills. It was only while drinking some water to wash them down - with his glass - that she felt an odd sense of dislocation. How long had it been since she had sipped from a cup or glass?

She spread the cream along her furrow, wincing slightly, then replaced it and awkwardly climbed back from the counter to the chair and then to the floor. She put the chair back in place and crawled back to the hall, stopping in annoyance to work at the straps binding her ankles back. She could neither slide them off nor undo them, and wondered resentfully how much of her meekness was due to being forced to crawl like an animal almost every day. It certainly affected the way one thought. Still, there was nothing she could do about it, so muttering, she continued on.

Her stomach rumbled a bit, but it always seemed to be empty of late. She never really got a lot of food, or at least, not good food. He seemed to feed her mostly junk. Feeling indignant she turned and crawled back to the kitchen, then opened the refrigerator and got herself a banana, which she devoured gratefully. Then, daring still further, she plucked down a carton of milk and drank from it.

Feeling somewhat sated she crawled back up the hall to his office. She saw no sign of calendars, and climbed up onto his big chair before his desk, looking through his mail. She found a few pieces that looked new and checked the postmarks. It was the fourth of March. She had arrived in New York mid-January. It had been two weeks or so before she met with Richardson, so she had been with him for about a month now.

'A month!?' she exclaimed. Where on earth had the time gone? She had thought it more like a week. Had it really been four weeks? Surely not. She frowned as she stared at the postmark, then something caught her attention and she realised it had been mailed in London. That brought another swarm of images to her swirling mind and curiously she opened it, and frowned at the distinctive handwriting.

It was handwriting she knew well, for it was her stepfather's handwriting.

I am, of course, pleased with how events have come to pass, but as I have informed you on several occasions the photocopies of my stepdaughter's relinquishment of her financial affairs to me are insufficient for authorities here in London. I require the actual notarised forms she has signed. As to your desire for a larger fee for your efforts I will, of course, consider them once the statements have been turned over to me. I ask you to consider, however, that your efforts have not been unrewarded by me thus far, and that from the videos you have forwarded it is apparent this work involves considerable benefits in and of itself.

Gwen stared at the writing, squinting to make out the words. She was kneeling on the chair, elbows propped on the desktop as she read, frowning in confusion and disbelief. At first she could not understand how her stepfather had ever even come to know about Richardson, then she struggled to understand what he meant about relinquishing her financial affairs. She hadn't signed anything...

Or had she? She had made so many statements to video and tape recorders, and written and signed so many lurid descriptions of things she had done, or even fantasised about. But he had always torn those up, hadn't he?

What on earth was going on?

The desk was locked, as were the cabinets behind it. She angrily considered breaking them open, but did not dare. Instead she searched the house, but quickly came to the conclusion that the only place in it Richardson would hide anything incriminating - unless he had a hidden safe she knew nothing about - was in his office.

She did find, however, some interesting reading material in his bedside table. It was a book on mind control. Among passages underlined were those advising to keep the subject thirsty and not let them have too much in the way of protein, to keep them from getting any decent sleep, and to constantly reinforce the behaviour considered improper with punishment. It spoke of something called subliminal assimilation, in which constantly repeated orders at barely audible levels would imprint themselves on the subject's mind.

'That filthy, miserable bastard!' she cursed vehemently, embracing her opinion of both men with one outburst.

Had she really signed a document turning her financial affairs over to her stepfather? If she had it meant nothing at that moment. But when her grandparents' trust fund came due in a few months it would mean quite a bit, to say the least! Of course, once she showed up she could simply rescind the thing.

Once she showed up.

If she showed up!

Such a document would be useless in her presence, for she would simply disavow it. If she were absent for an extended period, however, her stepfather could make whatever use of her money he desired.

She needed more information about what the two of them were planning, and turned to Richardson's computer. Fortunately it required no password to enter and she snorted angrily at his obvious contempt for her ability, or perhaps her desire to figure out what was going on. She quickly looked for any files of his own making. There were many, but she limited herself to those no more than a month old.

That left a much narrower field to search and she found it in a small sub-directory called *Slave*. Inside were a number of letters he had sent to her stepfather. Most were replies to letters most likely locked in his desk. The first spoke of her, of finding her in a club and watching her go home with some young man, and stated that he thought there would be little difficulty in enticing her to his penthouse.

Each letter seemed to grow more and more smug, and Richardson obviously enjoyed taunting her stepfather with the sexual details of how he was 'training' his sluttish stepdaughter. Her face grew red with anger and embarrassment as she read through them, barely able to credit the thought that he had actually mailed the things to her stepfather.

...seemed to feel being buggered was somewhat beneath her status in life, but she quickly grew to love it. Of course she put up a token resistance at first, but was soon begging me for more. Some girls are naturals in that way, you know...

'My God,' she whispered, putting a hand over her mouth. Murderous thoughts crossed her mind, but far more urgent was locating any remaining videos or signed statements; aside from her inheritance, the humiliation she felt at the thought of people she knew viewing videos of her or reading her fantasies was almost unbearable.

She needed the keys to the desk and those cabinets. It was possible she could break into them without, if she could find hammers or pry bars, but they were strongly built, and if she failed there was no hiding what she was after and no telling what he would do to her. He and her stepfather obviously could not let her go home again if they were to share out her trust fund, so what were they going to do with her?

She would have to get his keys when he was home, asleep, most likely. The problem with that notion was that he never left her unbound when he was home, except when she was caged. And he didn't always let her sleep in the cage. She had not realised why until she scanned the book on mind control techniques. Obviously he did not want her getting any decent sleep. Having seven or eight full hours might clear her mind enough to wonder at her captivity.

So usually she was bound in a position of some discomfort, sometimes simply standing up all night. When she slept it was usually for a period of an hour or two during the day or evening. In this way she was constantly a little fuzzy, and keeping her protein intake low and smacking her whenever she spoke or acted out of turn seemed to have robbed her of whatever rebellious thoughts she might have held.

No, that wasn't entirely true, she told herself. She had revelled in the sexual degradation, in the use and abuse, in being ravished and treated like a sexual animal. It was that as much as anything else that had kept her from rebelling.

Even reading his taunting letters to her father she felt a quiver of arousal at being so degraded, at the memory of the activities he described.

...seems to be a natural whore... one letter said. *...I'm sure you would have been pleased with her the other evening when she performed sexually with six of my male acquaintances. She climaxed so enthusiastically a few of them thought she was playacting; that no woman could be so wanton...*

Gwen remembered the occasion. It had both embarrassed and exhilarated her to be naked in front of six strangers, fully dressed older men, and to present herself to each for a spanking and then to be used as they chose. She felt her loins warming at the memory, at the images of herself and the men involved.

She shook her head as if to clear it and then considered her options.

The best would probably be to find something to cut through the leather straps, find something to wear and then take a taxi to... well, to anywhere.

But she was not about to call her stepfather for money home. She couldn't - not now.

No, she was going to find whatever evidence Richardson had against her, and...

Gwen frowned as she came across some new information in Richardson's computer. It was regarding a new mining company he was organising with others, including her stepfather. That, apparently, was how the two men had become acquainted. She knew little about business, but knew quite a bit about stocks. Her trust was largely in stocks, after all, and she had greedily followed them for some time.

She frowned as she read through the file, then the others that accompanied it. She had to puzzle quite a few things out at first, but gradually she understood they were discussing a highly illegal stock swindle. The men had formed a mining company - on paper. They were discussing how to build the company up by word of mouth and rumour before it opened on the stock exchange. The company was supposed to be laid out as one hastily formed to take advantage of

107

an enormous gold find in Indonesia. Those with the 'inside scoop' would be able to buy up the stock quickly and then make a fortune when it skyrocketed as the news was released.

Except that there was no company and no gold mine.

Gwendolyn Allison Pepperdine smirked to herself as the details of a plan formed in her mind.

Chapter 14

'Grovel, you slut!'

Gwen panted as she crawled frantically along the hall trying to escape the lash of Richardson's switch, hearing the laughter of his two companions as they herded her towards the dungeon. She had already performed oral sex on all three men, but that was merely the warm up, and a part of her trembled with suppressed excitement at the anticipation of what they would do to her next.

It had been several days since she found out about Richardson's plan, but she had not yet been able to do anything. Richardson had taken to shackling her in place as often as using the leather restraints. It was apparently easier and he was growing more complacent about his use of her. The locks on the shackles were simple affairs, for they were made more for play than for seriously restraining prisoners. The keys to many were interchangeable.

She had managed to take one such key, a small thing little larger than her thumbnail, and somehow contrived to hang on to it, hiding it in her mouth, tucked beneath her tongue.

But he never shackled her at any time when he was asleep or out. He used the tighter leather restraints with their unreachable buckles. She knew she was running out of time, for sooner or later he would find the little handcuff key and then she would be in real trouble. Worse still, she was starting to have lapses where she forgot what she was planning or even why. Even hating him as much as she did she still found her body responding to his touch, to his punishments and restraining methods, even to his presence. Her mind was sinking again into the role of compliant sexual slave ever ready to please and obey her master.

The key was safely under her tongue, and she had developed the skill of keeping it there even when having to fellate a man, which she just had - three of them.

Richardson turned to her and unceremoniously dragged her up to her feet by the hair, then placed her between two beams and raised her arms. He spread them apart and clipped her leather wrist restraints to chains in the beams, forcing her to stand very straight.

Then he picked up a strange U-shaped metal pipe and carried it back to her. He laid the legs down on the floor then pushed it into her lower abdomen, forcing her feet to shift backwards. The cold steel pushed harder and he eased the lower legs into two postholes set in the floor, and then gave a final shove.

The effect was to push her hips back from the beams, which meant her bottom jutted back and she was forced to bend forward a little, rising to her toes. Her bottom was thus perfectly posed for any use they cared to make of it.

'I ask you, gentlemen, is this not a magnificent bottom?' he boasted.

'It truly is,' one of the men replied.

'Yes, gorgeous,' the other said, nodding sagely.

Hands moved across her bottom, squeezing and lightly slapping.

'This is a backside made for punishment,' Richardson said.

Gwen moaned softly and he slapped her bottom again, sniggering contemptuously. 'The slut knows what she likes,' he said.

He was a *real* snake. And yet her pussy was starting to thrum excitedly and her breathing was growing more ragged - and it grew worse when he grinned at her and displayed an odd looking little metal triangle. One side held a narrow strip of some material that looked like suede. He reached beneath the horizontal bar pressed against her abdomen, and she felt that side of the triangle pushing up against her pussy. Then it snapped into place on the underside of the bar and she moaned anew at the pressure it exerted, pushing up firmly against her clit.

Richardson moved away, then returned, holding a crude plastic phallus. He fed it into her pussy, working it in slowly but not terribly gently, he and the other men sniggering at her distress as it penetrated deep into her body.

A pair of weights was then clipped to her nipples, and the men were ready to get started.

Richardson offered the first go to the thinner of the two guests, and he picked up a strap, positioned himself to one side of her and swung it horizontally.

Crack!

Gwen groaned as it struck her bottom. The pain was not great, but the impact made her jerk helplessly. Her groin jammed against the suede strip and her pussy clenched sharply around the thick dildo inside.

The heat of the blow had barely begun to subside when another followed, then another, then another still. The man rained abuse on her as he strapped her, asking how she liked it and if she knew how much she deserved it.

Her bottom grew blotchy and hot and her groin began heaving more purposefully against the strip between her legs. She told herself not to - told herself she must resist. Several times she almost lost control, forgot completely about the key and almost let it slip from her mouth.

Her bottom was aflame when the man stopped, and then the second stranger moved in, holding a long switch. The blow was sharper, lighter, yet more painful, the sting deeper and more acute. She yelped and jerked more violently, gasping and panting as she tried to hold herself still. The pleasure grew and the sexual haze began to cloud her mind.

So what if he kept her there forever? She'd be a real slave then - a sexual prisoner!

She ground herself against the strip angled so perfectly in beneath her and squeezed her vaginal muscles around the thick intruder wedged there. The thinner man reached in and slapped the base of the dildo that protruded from her, and she cried out as her body was thrown forward. The switch bit into her soft buttocks, angling lower, snapping at the top of her thighs, and she whimpered and squirmed in a vain attempt to avoid its bite.

Then Richardson set to work with a riding crop. The blow was heavier now, and the pain had much more bite to it. She cried out with each strike, tears filling her eyes as the pain mounted. Again and again she was driven off her toes to hang there against the bar wedged into her abdomen, the angled strip jammed in hard against her clitoris.

One of the men moved forward in his eagerness and opened his trousers. With one lunge he thrust himself into her bottom, rutting furiously, jamming her sex against the strip of material wedged there and driving her into an incredible climax. Only chance stopped her from swallowing the key or it dropping from her slack lips as her mind disintegrated under the maelstrom of sensory exultation. She spasmed and jerked as his groin pummelled her ravaged buttocks and his hands mauled her breasts.

He finished with her and stepped back, and Richardson struck her with a cane. Her head rolled back and she just had the presence of mind to embed the key safely under her tongue again as a little sanity returned with the pain, and held it there as another blow followed, then another, and still more. She was sobbing openly, tears dropping to the floor below, but none of the men appeared to feel any pity for her.

The second stranger moved behind her and penetrated her bottom, and when he was finished Richardson took his turn, using her as roughly as always as he forced her into another climax.

And it was glorious.

Again she told herself she did not care if she remained his prisoner forever, did not care if he passed her around to friends and acquaintances, to be bound and beaten and fucked endlessly. What a sensuous, hedonistic life that would be!

But the sexual haze retreated as he finished, and as they set her down. She tried to comfort her aching, burning bottom, but this drew nothing but laughter as her arms were lifted behind her and attached to the ring set in the back of her collar, and she was led to a new frame she'd not seen before. For some reason it reminded her of the sharply angled roof to a well or doghouse, sitting on a pair of blocks. It was roughly waist high, and Richardson and one of his guests lifted her up on top, forcing her to straddle the thing, spreading her legs wide.

The straps fastened her legs to each side at thigh and ankle, and then while one of the men bound her hair in a tail the other fed two narrow wires from the wall in front of the frame to the rings in her nipples. She grunted, leaning forward, thrusting her chest up in an attempt to ease the pain. A moment later her ponytail was pulled, arching her head and shoulders back.

The thin wedge at the top of the frame pressed into her pussy lips, forcing them apart, and leaning forward to ease the pull on her breasts dropped all her weight directly on her sensitive pink flesh. She whimpered softly, easing a little way back, but this stretched her nipples even more painfully.

'Have a little rest now, Gwendolyn,' Richardson said, clearly amused. 'We'll get back to you.'

At first, though the pressure between her legs was heavy, the pain was quite tolerable. However, every minute her weight rested on the delicate flesh of her mons the pain grew worse, a powerful throbbing which spread throughout her groin and up into her abdomen. It grew and grew until it became unbearable, and she found herself sobbing and moaning, trying to roll from side to side or back or forth to somehow lift herself free from the terrible pressure.

But it was hopeless. She could do nothing but sit there straddling the awful frame, crying with anguish and frustration.

It was much worse than when she was hung by the elderly Japanese man - although that was bad enough - for the rope was flexible and moulded to her body, whereas the wood was immoveable and pressed directly against her pussy. It was such a simple device, and yet so horrible, something clearly made with the female body in mind, and she felt a black rage at the thought of Richardson placing her upon it, giving her such terrible anguish simply for his amusement and the amusement of his pathetic sycophants.

And when she considered that the whole idea was her stepfather's that rage grew even more intense. She thought of him lounging back comfortably in his leather armchair at the club sipping his aperitif as he read the paper, wearing that smug expression - the one that always made her want to slap him.

And here she was, tears spilling from her eyes. And if he knew would he be... no, she could not even contemplate *that*. And yet she could not keep the awful thought from seeping into her tormented mind: would he be... turned on?

Gwen shook her head, trying to rid herself of the ghoulish thought, more salty tears meandering down her red cheeks as she did.

After an interminable time Richardson returned alone, smiling at her angst. But he did release her and let her lay in the cage to recover, wrists bound behind her back, planning violent retribution on him and her stepfather.

She dozed a little, having no idea what time it was.

He left her there for an indeterminate time, then returned and made her crawl back to the main front room for no apparent reason; he had her stand against a pillar as he read the newspaper, her wrists shackled to the wall above her head as she sagged weakly. And then she realised angrily that it was another ploy to prevent her getting too much rest.

Once he had read all he wanted of the newspaper he took her to the bathroom and watched quietly while she showered and dried herself, and she savoured the opportunity to let the steaming water and fragrant shower gel soothe her aching limbs. Once dried he led her, crawling on all fours, to his large bed and handcuffed her wrists together to a ring set high in one of the four posts that supported the canopy. He pushed a gag into her mouth and then prepared for bed.

If he had seen the sparkle of anticipation in her eyes he would have been considerably less relaxed and would not have fallen asleep as easily as he did. Gwen stood as still as possible, watching him in the darkness, waiting, heart pounding every time she thought about taking the key from her mouth, sure it was a trap; that somehow he knew all about her plans and was just laying in wait for her.

Hours passed, and still she did not dare move. Then finally she raised a foot and placed it carefully on the frame of the bed. Her hands tightened on the post as she slowly and gently raised herself up. She held still, staring at his motionless shape, listening to his even breathing, then arched to inch her mouth close to her open hand. She took the key carefully in her fingers, worked it into the lock, and with a soft click her pulse raced and the handcuffs parted.

She stepped down very slowly and then dropped to her knees, listening to his breathing. When there was no change she crawled around to the chair where he had left his trousers. She reached into one pocket and her fingers closed around the thick chain of keys he always carried, making sure every key was clamped tightly in the palm of her hand so they would not jangle as she drew them forth. She started to move away, then hesitated, withdrew his wallet and removed all the bills before replacing it.

With keys and money in hand she crawled towards and then through the half open door, not rising to her feet until she was well along the hall.

Her heart pounded as she headed for his office. Even now she half suspected he was simply waiting for her, and that he would appear from out of the shadows and drag her to the torture room for punishment.

She closed his office door and turned on the light, then hurried to the desk. She tried several keys before finding the right one, and then carefully opened the drawers, one by one, as quietly as possible, keeping her ears alert for any sound of movement from outside the office.

In the top right-hand drawer she found a bundle of letters from her stepfather. The first informed Richardson of his problems with his recalcitrant stepdaughter, and his worries about her wasting the inheritance she would soon receive. He spoke about her weakness and lack of morality and wondered in writing what might be done about her.

Underneath the bundle were all the 'confessions' she had made and Richardson had supposedly ripped up. Along with them were statements about the sexual activities she had participated in and fantasies she allegedly held; and worse, at the bottom of the drawer, was a legal document giving her stepfather power of attorney and control of her funds. It alarmed her to think she simply could not recall writing such things.

She turned on Richardson's computer and printed the letters outlining his plans for the stock swindle and its timetable, cringing and eyeing the door anxiously while the printer clunked and whirred as it fed her the evidence she needed.

Next she unlocked the cabinets behind the desk. Most contained liquor, documents, and supplies, but one entire shelf contained video tapes, dozens of them, all marked with a number system she did not understand. She cursed and went to the door, then hurried along the hall to the storage cupboard she knew was there. She took a suitcase down from a shelf and returned, then took every one of the tapes, packing them in tightly.

She turned off the computer, locked the cabinet, and then returned to the drawers. She noticed a brown envelope in the bottom of the one that had contained her stepfather's letters and picked it out. Inside were a half-dozen letters from men in foreign countries, offering bids of twenty to twenty-five thousand dollars for his 'product'. Most were vague about the nature of it, but one, a man from Columbia, offered his money with the proviso that: *her breasts are genuine and not artificially enhanced.*

'Son of a *bitch*,' Gwen whispered, realisation dawning.

She took the envelope and stuck it in the suitcase, along with the other documents and letters, then locked the desk again. She wasn't sure why. She had some vague notion that he would not notice anything missing, but to make that work she would have had to return the keys to his trouser pockets, and she could not bring herself to dare enter his bedroom again.

Instead she went quietly to the small laundry room, looking for one of the less revealing dresses he'd purchased for her, but she found none, nor any of the lingerie, nor the clothes she had been wearing when she had arrived.

But at least her own coat was still hanging by the lift with her shoes placed neatly beneath it. She stared at his bedroom door, heart pounding, wondering whether to go back in and find some more comprehensive clothing, but in the end she made a hushed telephone call for a cab, her eyes anxiously scanning the enveloping shadows the whole time, put on her coat and shoes and took the lift down.

The cab arrived and she threw the suitcase inside, and then had him drive her to a motel. There she sat on the edge of the bed for hours, thinking, with the television on in the background for company. There had been only a pair of fifties and a few smaller bills in Richardson's wallet, and most of it had gone on the motel room.

That left her in a predicament. She could not get home and had no money to stay in New York. Nor did she really know anyone she could turn to. Nor could she stay in the motel. Come morning he would know she must have left by cab, and with his apparent connections would very easily find out where she had been taken. She had to get money from somewhere quickly, and enough to get her home.

Gwen stayed as long as she dared, until she knew he must be awake and looking for her, then took the suitcase and left. She walked for a dozen blocks before getting directions to the subway, and then took that to the railway station.

There she tried the key to the locker where she had left her things, but found it empty.

She went to the lost and found office and gave them most of the rest of her money as a fine and storage charge, desperately thankful that he had overlooked collecting her things as he said he would, then put on some clothes in a toilet, put both suitcases into another locker, and disappeared back onto the streets.

Gwen spent some time wandering, then looked up the address of the lesbian club in the phone book and took the subway there. With some difficulty - and a little sexual favour given to the girl behind the reception desk - she managed to extract the telephone number of Ms Brook, and luckily got hold of April directly with her first call. Having only just arisen she was still a little groggy, and could not remember the name of the escort agency she had spoken of before that specialised in bondage and SM. But she agreed to check up and give it to her.

Gwen then wandered aimlessly through streets and shops, killing time, and then called again. April gave her the address of the place and promised to tell no one, especially Richardson if he called and started asking questions.

Despite her recent experiences the thought of going there was making Gwen feel sick with nerves. But she saw little alternative. She needed money immediately, hundreds of dollars at least. She had to get a place to stay, and had to get a machine to view the tapes. She had no intention of getting on a plane with a suitcase overflowing with smutty tapes and risk having some nosy customs officer discover them.

Besides, hadn't she experienced everything these types could do to her? What difference would one or two more little experiences make?

It would be prostitution for one thing, she thought, but summoned her resolve and headed for the address April had given her. It was a small office in a large tower block of offices, and the sign on the door read *Daedes Consulting*.

A middle-aged woman looked up from her desk and frowned. 'Yes?' she challenged warily.

'I need to make some money quickly,' Gwen told her, deciding frankness was the best approach.

'Don't we all,' the woman retorted sarcastically. 'So what?'

'I was given this address,' Gwen said, holding out the scrap of paper upon which she'd written the details given her by April.

The woman pulled a face of disinterest, but at that moment a man emerged from a side room. He was pretty ordinary, wearing jeans and a sweatshirt.

'Who's this?' he asked, with about as much interest and warmth as the woman had shown - very little.

'Says she heard she could make some quick money here,' the woman informed him, without taking her sceptical stare from Gwen.

'Yeah, right,' he said aggressively. 'Get lost, honey.'

'I know what you do here and I need the money,' Gwen insisted hastily.

'And what do you think we do here?' the woman challenged.

'I think you hire out girls for sex,' Gwen said firmly.

'Oh, you think so, do you?' the woman sneered. 'And that's what you want to do, is it?'

'Well, I do need money,' Gwen confessed.

'So, you want us to take you on and rent you out to our clients, do you?' the woman laughed dismissively.

'Well, why don't you take off your clothes and show us what you've got?' the man suggested with a salacious smirk.

The woman laughed again. 'Yeah, why don't you do just that, eh, honey?'

Gwen despised the pair and what they were putting her through, but she opened and removed her coat as the woman sat back in her chair and the man perched on the edge of the desk, both devouring her with their eyes. Then, as casually as she could she took off her blouse, undid and lowered her skirt, and stepped out of her shoes.

She removed her bra and panties and stood with her back straight and her chin held proudly high, desperately trying to appear comfortable under their vulgar scrutiny.

'Turn around, show us everything,' the man ordered.

Gwen obeyed.

'Now bend over and grab your ankles.'

Heart in her mouth, face red, she obeyed, and cringed as the woman sniggered behind her.

'She's no cop,' the man decided, and the woman reluctantly grunted her agreement. 'So you need money, huh?' he went on. 'Okay, let's see how much you need it. Come here, on your knees.'

Gwen knew exactly what he would want from her, but she obeyed.

'You've done the bondage scene before?' he asked.

Gwen nodded. 'Some,' she said grudgingly.

'But you've never done prostitution work before, have you?' She shook her head, and as he gazed down at her kneeling before him he unfastened his jeans, pulled down the zipper, and drew out his semi-erect penis. 'Suck me,' he demanded.

He seemed to suffer no embarrassment at the presence of the woman, but Gwen could not say the same. Nevertheless she had no alternative, so she slipped her lips around his cock and began to suck. Her hands massaged his testicles, and then she took them into her mouth one by one as her fingers milked his cock.

He hardened even more and she began bobbing her lips up and down his length, then, wanting to impress him, she pushed forward, taking him to the back of her throat.

'Nice,' he grunted. '*Very* nice.'

The woman shifted a little and her chair creaked, but the only other sounds in the musty little room were the wet suckling noises of Gwen's lips and tongue, and the occasional hushed words of encouragement from the man. He guided the movements of her head with one hand, becoming more and more erratic, and gripped the edge of the desk with the other, and when he came she felt a great sense of relief that the ordeal was over and she had hopefully passed their sordid little test.

'Very good,' he decided, looking at the woman. 'They'll love her.'

The woman grinned slyly. 'Well, I'll need to decide that for myself,' she said. 'Come here, slut.'

Gwen started to rise from her knees but the man pushed her back down. 'Crawl,' he ordered, so she edged unwillingly over to the woman, who pushed her chair back from the desk and gripped Gwen's hair, roughly pulled her up across her lap and fingered her pussy.

'What a nasty little slut, coming here offering to prostitute herself,' she said, and then slapped Gwen's bottom hard, making her yelped with shock and pain. 'So, tell us what you've done,' she demanded, and slapped her bottom again.

The couple had Gwen dress in a black business suit, with a tailored jacket and white blouse that hugged her breasts and short skirt that hugged her bottom. Her hair was pulled back into a tight ponytail, and her own high heels and a pair of false horn-rimmed glasses and a briefcase completed her outfit. They provided her with a price list, and gave her the details for her first assignment that afternoon.

The client, Mr Marx, would pay in cash, they said, because he liked to avoid the documentation of a credit card transaction.

'Remember, you're playing a role,' the woman warned her. 'Make sure you act real bitchy; he likes to play rough. 'Just remember the money, and remember everything he does to you because it all costs separately.'

An older man greeted Gwen at the door of the address she was given and she decided she should get into her role from the outset, so she cleared her throat and scowled, looking him up and down with disdain.

'Are you Mr Marx?' she demanded.

He nodded and replied, 'Yes.'

'I'm here for your appointment,' she said severely, and walked in without being asked, brushing past him brusquely as he closed the front door.

'This way,' he said, indicating a door a little along the hall, and as soon as they were inside and the door was closed he thrust her against the side of a desk with such unexpected force that she dropped the briefcase and yelped with shock. He then shoved her between the shoulders, pinning her down against the desktop and knocking her glasses off. Then he yanked up her skirt while keeping his other hand on her neck, seized her panties and tore them off her with one violent tug.

'Spread your legs,' he hissed.

'Let me go, you pig!' Gwen cursed, but he merely slapped her bottom and she shrieked.

'Spread your legs, I said,' he repeated vehemently. 'I'll show you what you're here for!'

Gasping, she obeyed, felt his fingers clumsily probing her sex and whimpered as they pushed into her. But she had only a moment to contemplate the speed of the onslaught before the fingers disappeared and he impaled her with one frenetic lunge of his cock, his other hand keeping her cheek pinned to the desk.

As he set about fucking Gwen her knees knocked against the side of the desk and her breasts crushed against its surface with every rabid lunge, but she was otherwise able to endure it while he came quickly, shuddering and grunting as he stood behind her, glued to the shapely contours of her bare buttocks, pale in the gloom of the room.

Belying his older and fragile appearance, Mr Marx then pulled her limp wrists into the small of her back and tied them together with some lengths of soft fabric, and the force of his treatment secretly thrilled her.

He roughly dragged her up by the collar of the blouse, spun her round, then grabbed the front of the blouse and ripped it open, sending buttons popping and clattering to the floor. Then as Gwen struggled to recover from the sheer speed and surprise of the attack he gripped her bra, pulled it up, and started to maul and slobber over her naked breasts.

'Nice tits, for a lawyer,' he leered. Gwen gawped at him for a moment, chest tight with suppressed excitement, then recalled her role.

'You filthy pig,' she cursed. 'I'll... I'll file a complaint!'

'Ha! Complain all you want, slut!' he challenged, and then shoved her into the high-backed leather desk chair. 'Sit down!'

He bent and picked up a handful of leather straps. A moment later he was pushing them over her head and down over her face, forming a hood of sorts, buckling under her jaw. She tried to call him another name but he fed a small dildo between her lips, which filled her mouth as he strapped it in place, effectively gagging her.

He glared up at her as he squatted and snatched off her shoes, and then quickly lifted her feet, setting them on the seat, her heels pressed against her buttocks.

More leather straps bound her ankles firmly in place to the arms of the chair and he moved behind her, and she gasped as he reached down and gripped her under the arms, lifted her up, and dragged her over the back of the chair and down, bending her excruciatingly, and all she could do was whimper into the gag.

There was a metal ring set in the straps across her head and he slipped a chain through it then pulled down hard, securing it to the bottom of the chair.

'Slut,' he snarled.

Her back ached fiercely, for she was arched tautly over the top of the rounded chair back. Her head and torso were upside down, her lower half bound in place, legs spread. But despite the outrageous liberties he was taking and his rough treatment of her, Gwen felt wildly excited.

The skirt was stretched across the tops of her thighs - until he removed it, and as a hand mauled between her legs she moaned in abandoned excitement.

Mr Marx then walked around her, opened a cupboard, removed a whip, and then moved into position beside the chair and the lovely bound girl tensed over its back.

Being upside down, her head bound in place, she had a poor view of things, but she did see him raise the whip, draw it back and then swing it down. It lashed across her belly with a crack and she screamed.

He cursed her and lashed it down again, harder this time, then again across her abdomen. She winced and grunted, but felt a growing heat and need, her body seething with sexual electricity.

The whip swung down again, a dozen strips of leather spreading out to lash her taut belly, stinging her in a dozen places, and as the strips stung her lower abdomen she felt a desperate eagerness to feel them strike lower still.

But instead it moved higher and her breasts erupted with pain as the whip cut across them, and she wailed into the gag and writhed tormentedly as the chair creaked beneath her.

Again the whip descended, the individual strips stinging her breasts like a handful of little needles, biting into her rigid nipples.

But the pleasure was still the greater, increasing all the time. She was completely helpless at the hands of the cruel man, and who knew what he was capable of? She felt like a real prisoner, a real victim, and her body shuddered as her sexual anticipation intensified.

Then the whip returned across her lower chest, her belly and abdomen, and finally she felt the flexible strands curling under to snap at her exposed sex. She screamed again, pulling feebly at the restraining straps, but could barely move an inch as the stings erupted along her inner thighs and against her vulnerable sex.

Gwen could not see him, but something was pressed into her - another dildo. It pumped in and out and then was pushed deep and left in place as the whip rained down again, across her breasts and belly before dropping to her sex.

'You'll learn your place, slut,' he growled, striking her again and again.

Gwen came powerfully, gurgling and grunting and moaning into the gag as her body was ripped through by exquisite convulsions.

Chapter 15

Gwen smiled as the bell chimed to end the period. The professor gave a final series of reminders regarding homework and the class gathered up its books, rose, and headed for the door.

She had a new interest in financial matters, and was doing very well in the courses she was taking. In addition she had enrolled in acting classes, and was taking lessons in massage.

Of course, those were just a few of the classes she was taking. She intended to thoroughly familiarise herself with every facet of finance and investments, and then take a few law courses for good measure. Then there were the hair and beauty tips from modelling lessons, more art history, political science, and psychology.

Not all clients were as easy to please as Mr Marx, and she was slowly building a reputation for great style in her role-playing that was making her much in demand amongst London's hedonistic elite. She did not consider herself a prostitute, though she charged extremely large amounts for every 'consultation' with her clients; she did not need the money, after all; her trust fund had been turned over to her on her twenty-first birthday and contained more than enough to keep her in good style for the rest of her life.

What her clients saw in her was obvious; a lovely, uninhibited young woman who let them behave in a manner few other women would.

That she enjoyed it all was something few of them understood. That she was in such a business to please herself would have astonished them. She accepted clients when she chose to, which was dependant upon her own needs and desires.

And those needs and desires were considerable, for what Richardson had awakened in her had shown now sign of fading. She revelled in her own submissiveness. And since men were evidently willing to pay for the honour of dominating her she saw no reason to grant them her favours for free.

She'd never had any idea what she wanted to do with her life, but now thanks to Richardson and, she supposed, her stepfather, she did. She even had plans to open her own agency one day soon. After she had finished all her courses and built up a large enough client base she would recruit a couple of girls she could put through college and have learn massage, art, finance, and all the other subjects needed to please a discerning client.

And she would teach them all those other things discerning clients required and would pay for, and teach them to love it. She had almost every minute of her own training at Richardson's home on video tape to consult should she need to. And some of it was truly inspired.

Oh, she had no need to twist their impressionable minds by force, but if on viewing a few of them a girl didn't grasp the pleasure and eroticism to be found in submission, well, she would know she had the wrong girl.

Yes, she owed her stepfather and Richardson a great deal. It was really rather ironic that their lessons had wound up bankrupting them. Having borrowed every penny they could and put every pound and dollar into their phoney scheme they'd managed to build the stock up quite well. Unfortunately, copies of their plans and correspondence had turned up on the desks of financial reporters in New York and London before they could get their money out. Not only had they lost everything, but also both were facing charges of fraud and misappropriation.

It really was a pity. Perhaps, once she got her business well and truly off the ground, she'd offer them a discount or two while her girls were training. It would have to be a very steep discount, given their current poverty, but then she was a generous girl.

Gwen stood up, the little dildo secretly buried inside her pussy making her gasp softly. She smoothed down her sweater, her hand passing surreptitiously over the rings impaling her nipples beneath the soft fabric, then picked up her books and made her way out of the classroom and up the stairs.

Education wasn't so very boring, after all.

Also by John Argus and available as a paperback on AMAZON

'Shhh,' he cajoled, then drew her forward between a pair of waist high posts. Each had a brass ring at its top, and a thin chain attached. He drew her right arm out to one side and attached a shackle to it. Leah felt her stomach lurch and opened her mouth to protest; yet no sound emerged. She jerked her arm back, but no real conviction was behind it. And then her other wrist was shackled to the opposite post and her heart was beating like a trip hammer as he moved away to one corner, and maneuvered a tall, antique, gold embossed mirror in front of her, cocked at a slight angle. Her reflected eyes were enormous and her expression stricken. She could see the outline of her erect nipples through her thin blouse, and her cheeks began to flush as she became aware of his scrutiny.

They hunt the shadows of the night, spoken of only in rumors and whispers. Vampires: ancient and powerful, creatures of magic who hunger for flesh and blood. Detective Leah MacInnes is tough, beautiful, and thinks she's seen it all.

Girls are going missing, but Leah can hardly concentrate on the case because her new boss is a tough, cold lesbian whom she hates... and wants. So she roams the streets and clubs at night, giving herself to strange men in a desperate attempt to ease the desire gripping her body and soul.

And in the depths of darkness each night a ghostly figure takes her, punishes her, and promises her she will come to him, kneel at his feet, and call him master...